SWORD OF BALM AND SHADOW

COURT OF BLOOD AND BINDING BOOK 3

MAGGIE ALABASTER

TRIGGER WARNING

Chapter 7 contains a scene of sexual assault. It's contained to that chapter, with another warning as a reminder. This chapter can be skipped without losing any elements of the story.

1

KHALA

I stepped out of the portal to the sight of the Spring Court palace.

Stark, white marble was formed into the shape of a giant lotus. Massive petals sat half-open, ready to greet the sun. At dawn, it would be tinged pink. At sunset, red and gold.

I might have been impressed if I was here voluntarily.

I shook my head, trying in vain to dislodge Wornar's alpha-order from my mind. It was lodged harder than Dalyth's block in Zared's mind. Heavy and unyielding.

I hated it, hated *him*.

Wornar.

Cousin and heir of the High Lord of the Spring Court.

Cavan's blood was still wet on my hand. Red stained my sleeve. The image of him falling to the ground played over and over in my mind. The knife embedded in his side. The knife slid in there by me, under Wornar's fucking order. Words that gave me no choice but to stab one of my lovers.

I wanted to stab Wornar. Wanted his blood to coat my hand. I wanted him to look me in the eyes as he died, knowing who held the knife.

My grudge was the heaviest thing I held right now, but I clung to it. Whatever happened, he'd regret what he made me do.

Tears ran down my cheeks. I let them. Maybe Wornar would feel bad if he saw them. Some hint of guilt at forcing me to shed Cavan's blood. A shred of remorse.

That seemed less than unlikely. He strode in front of me, chin raised, anything but repentant.

Fucking asshole.

On the other end of the bond, all four men were frantic. I sent back the plea I'd sent since the moment Wornar made me slide the knife between Cavan's ribs.

Help him. Go to the Autumn Court and stop him

from dying. I needed them to do that for me. If Cavan died...

Ryze sent back that they were on their way, then they were coming for me. Coming for Wornar. He sent reassurance, but also fear tinged with confusion as to what happened to Cavan.

The bond was good for sending emotions, but not solid information, not words. That they knew I was all right would have to be enough for now.

"I know you must be confused," Wornar said. "You'll understand soon enough." He smiled at me as if we were friends. "You can talk now if you like. We're safe here."

That part of the alpha-order lifted, a slight shift in weight, like loosening his grip around my throat.

I wanted to tell him to fuck off, but held my tongue. He was worth my rage, but not my words. After decades as a Silent Maiden, unable to speak, I'd learnt the value of not speaking. Often silence says more than the most eloquent speech.

He continued as though oblivious to my anger. "I'm sure you'll agree, all the conjecture about the other courts has done nothing but cause friction and conflict. We should be searching for a way to seal them off forever, not release them back into the world."

I was unable to contain my response. "That's a conversation for all of the High Lords," I said bitterly. "Not for just one to decide."

"Tell that to Ryze and Cavan," Wornar said easily, undeterred. "They didn't seem concerned about not consulting Harel or Thiron. Cavan even went so far as to take you into the Autumn Court to steal the key from Harel."

I shrugged. "The consensus seems to be the Court of Shadows and the Court of Dreams will find their way back, with or without our help. Ryze and Cavan wanted to do it while we were united enough to stand against them if they posed a threat."

Wornar stopped, turned around and faced me. "*If* they pose a threat? How many Fae have to die before they recognise that they *already* pose a threat?"

I stood my ground and stared him down. "They know there's a threat. Right now it's a small one. They want to stop it from becoming worse later." So far, we'd seen nothing more than random attacks and only one, arguably deserved, death. Dalyth.

Wornar stepped closer. We were almost chest to chest. "They won't be a threat if we seal them away forever. *When* we seal them away." He smelled of oak, alpha and determination, tainted with something else. Ambition and the burning desire to be right. To win against anyone who might think to stand in his way. The combination left a bitter sensation on my tongue.

Did the High Lord of the Spring Court know who he had in his midst? Wornar had fooled Ryze. The High Lord of the Winter Court considered him something close to a friend. The gods only knew what Thiron thought.

"Is that what you need me for?" I managed not to flinch.

He was so close I was sure I could hear his heartbeat. His harsh breath all but scraped the side of my face, rough like a desert breeze.

"Potentially." He brushed hair off my cheek and tucked it behind my ear. "We also need you to keep Ryze and Cavan from doing anything stupid. If they do, it won't end well for you."

"So I'm a hostage," I stated. Fuck. I shouldn't be too surprised. Why else would he bring me here?

"Of sorts," he agreed. "The Spring and Autumn Courts have one thing in common. Lack of omegas. That's something Thiron has been trying to rectify for quite some time. He's not going to want to let you go too easily. Fortunately, you'll like it here. The Spring Court is so much nicer than any of the others. You won't find all the dreary red and gold here. Or the ice, or the relentless summer."

"I'd rather be anywhere but here with you," I told him. If he thought anything different, he was delusional.

I didn't see the slap until my cheek was stinging from the impact. I was forced back a step. My hand flew to my face. I raised the other to hit back, but he grabbed my wrist and yanked me closer.

"You will never try to strike or hurt me in any way," he ordered. "Ever. You will obey me and Thiron, and any other alpha from the Spring Court. You'll watch what you say, or you can look forward to being a silent omega."

I closed my eyes and tried to ignore the order. Tried to stop it from wrapping itself around me and tying itself tight like a noose. So tight I could hardly breathe.

"Do you understand?" His nose almost touched mine. "You will respond with *yes, alpha*."

No matter how much I wanted to, I couldn't stop the words from leaving my lips. My whole body felt like it wasn't mine anymore. Like I was a shell for something darker.

"Good girl." He skated the back of his knuckle down my cheek. "One more thing. From now on, unless I say otherwise, pleasing me will be the only thing that will give you any satisfaction. Me and any other Spring Court alpha. That seems to have been missed in your training, somehow. My role is to take care of you, your role is to please me. Understand?"

"Yes, alpha," I said automatically. Inside, I felt like I was being torn in two. Part of me wanted to grab his sword and run him through with it. The rest of me wanted to get down on my knees and let him fuck my mouth.

Gods, this was worse than having the choker around my neck and not being able to talk. Then, I could communicate my honest thoughts and feelings. Now, I was in a battle with myself.

"Come with me." He let my wrist go and stepped back.

We made our way past a contingent of guards dressed in long tunics and fitted leather pants. Their tunics were either a soft green, or the blue of the spring sky. Each wore their pale red-gold hair long. They watched me with either blue eyes or green, tracking every step. Everyone was armed to the teeth.

They watched us as we walked past, gazes following, bodies tense and ready. They were a far cry from the indolent, disinterested guards from the

Autumn Court, or those from the Summer Court who seemed innately mistrustful of anyone from outside the court. The guards from the Winter Court were as arrogant and laid back as Ryze.

I thought Wornar would lead me to the throne room, but instead he led me to a wide chamber with a stone balcony that overlooked a stunning garden.

A Fae with a striking resemblance to Wornar stood near the railing, a heavy clay cup held in both hands. He didn't turn until we stepped out onto the balcony, and waited for at least a handful of minutes. He must have known we were there, but decided to deal with us when he was ready.

Finally, he turned to face his cousin. His blue eyes were striking. His glance bore into my soul.

He wore alphaness like a cloak. And smelled of it. As with Wornar, the scent of oak lingered on his skin, along with something else. Something between lavender and a spice I couldn't identify. It wasn't unpleasant, but it wasn't compelling either. Not exactly.

He didn't seem concerned about the blood on my skin and clothes.

When he finished drinking me with his eyes, his attention turned to Wornar.

"You got the key?"

"Not without a slight altercation, but I got it, yes. Once we destroy it, no one will be able to open Nallis." Wornar pulled the key out of his pocket and held it out on his palm.

Thiron looked at it for another long, slow moment, then nodded. That seemed to be the way he did things, slow and deliberate. Like the flower-dotted vine that wound its way up the side of the palace, and around the stone railing. It looked like it had been working to get there for a hundred years. The white flowers gave off a soft fragrance, in contrast with the two men.

I glanced off the balcony, to the stunning garden below. It was beautiful, a riot of colours and fragrances. Completely enclosed by a wall too high for me to climb. I wouldn't get out that way then.

"Good. We can work on a way to seal the courts." Thiron nodded. Slowly, of course. He looked like he was trapped in a vat of honey. Unable rather than unwilling to move quickly.

"I have good reason to believe she knows exactly where to find them." Wornar turned his blue eyes to me.

I really, really wanted to tell him to fuck off, but that was overridden with the need to tell him every-thing I knew. The words spilled out of my mouth.

"According to Ryze and Cavan, the best way to go is through Nallis," I said. "Otherwise, the only other way is through the mist. Ryze hated the mist. It scared him. He said he'd rather go through Nallis and some dark tunnel than go through the mist."

I hated myself for babbling all of that.

"Did he say why he didn't like it?" Thiron asked. He blinked at me, his long lashes brushing the tops of his cheeks. He'd be ridiculously handsome under other circumstances.

Had he told Wornar to bring me here? I assumed he had. Asshole until proven otherwise.

"He said he couldn't see where he was going," I said. "I always got the impression there was more to it, but he didn't say." It was the kind of thing he wouldn't elaborate on unless he was ready to. He was relieved when another way through the mountains presented itself.

Thiron's full lips drew back to the side in what looked like contemplation. "According to legend, people have tried to enter the mist and haven't returned."

"The mists engulf the side of a mountain," Wornar pointed out. "They probably couldn't see where they were going and fell to their deaths."

Thiron's gaze slowly swung towards him. For a

moment I thought he might suggest Wornar go find out. Instead, he nodded.

Shame, I supported sending Wornar to die.

"It's possible that was what occurred. It's also possible there's more there than an unlucky misstep."

"So the only way through is through Nallis," I concluded.

"This will require further thought and research," Thiron said. "In the meantime, no one will be able to enter Nallis. That may keep them from exacerbating the situation further."

I wanted to scream at them that wasn't how this was going to go. I'd seen the results of those portals opening and magic being thrown through. The Court of Shadows and the Court of Dreams weren't going to sit back and give up because Ryze, Cavan and the others couldn't take a shortcut to find them.

Wornar nodded and closed his fingers over the key. "I'll put this somewhere safe, until you're ready to have it destroyed." He didn't look sure that was what Thiron intended at all.

The order he put on me would keep me from stealing it a second time. Otherwise, that's what I'd do. Then I'd try again to make a portal and get the hells out of here. For Fae Ryze considered friends and allies, these two were anything but friendly and trustworthy.

"I'll get our guest settled," Wornar added.

Thiron nodded and turned his attention back to the garden.

"Follow me," Wornar snapped.

2

KHALA

I had no choice but to do what he said, but I didn't have to like it.

The order gave me enough freedom to turn back and look at Thiron. He looked like a man who had the weight of a thousand stars on his shoulders.

Strangely enough, he reminded me of Cavan. Maybe even Ryze. Both were trying to do what they thought was right for their court. For Jorius as a whole.

I hated to admit it, but I had no idea who was actually right in any of this. Maybe it was Thiron. Maybe we *should* find a way to stop the other courts from returning. Maybe in trying to free them, we'd bring about our own destruction.

One thing I knew for certain, Harel, High Lord of the Autumn Court, was wrong to sit back and do nothing. He wanted to believe the other courts didn't exist, that if he ignored them long enough, they might go away.

Wornar stepped back inside and I was forced to hurry to catch up to him.

"Ryze gave you absolutely no indication what he thought might be in the mist?" he asked. "Nothing at all?"

"Just that there was something." I shifted my shoulders, trying to see how far away from him I could get. No further than I was. Close enough that he could reach out his hand and touch me. "You must know I can't lie to you."

"I know if anyone could, it would be you," he said. "You're smart enough to find a way around the order, if there is one. Of course, I could order you not to lie to me."

"You're enjoying this, aren't you?" I asked. What was it with Fae men and the need to be controlling? Cavan enjoyed it too much when we were pretending I was broken. Now this.

I ignored the bond for the last while, but I felt for it now. The response was a jumble of confusion.

Something about working to get to Cavan and at the same time, needing to reach me. They seemed to be having trouble doing both of those things.

Zared was angry at everyone, but that was nothing new. Vayne was equally angry. It felt like Ryze was struggling to keep them and everything else together.

I sent thoughts that I was all right, then turned my attention from the bond.

"Why wouldn't I be enjoying it? I've been heir to the Spring Court for two hundred years. Do you know what that means?"

"It means you'll be High Lord some day?" That was technically correct, but I suspected he meant more than that.

"Some day," he said bitterly. "Some day that may be another two or three hundred years coming. And will only come if Thiron doesn't father a child."

"You're worried you'll never get to take over from him?" Honestly, being High Lord looked like a big pain in the ass to me. Far too much responsibility and hassle.

"I'm sure I will eventually," he said. "In the meantime, it means doing whatever he tells me to do. I speak on his behalf, but only with his permission."

He stopped at a door before pulling down the gilded handle and pushing it open. "Sometimes he doesn't override the things I've said or the decisions I've tried to make."

"Sometimes? Most of the time he does?" Did he think I gave a fuck?

I followed him into a sumptuous room decorated in dusky shades of pink, blue and yellow.

Gold thread was woven into plump cushions which sat neatly on the wide bed.

Mahogany and glass doors lead out to a balcony covered with potted plants, each full of scented flowers. The whole place smelled like lavender, roses and magnolia.

"Not directly." He closed the door behind us. "Usually he finds some sort of fault with whatever I do. He might as well tie my hands behind my back."

I started to say I didn't care, but the words wouldn't come.

Instead what came out was, "That seems tedious."

What was the point of making a decision when someone else would override it anyway? Hopefully he didn't mistake my words for sympathy. Whatever situation he was in, I didn't give a shit.

"I agree. He should trust me to advise him, and

listen to what I say. I'm the one who travels around Jorius speaking to people on his behalf. I know what the fuck is going on."

Wornar stalked out to the balcony and snapped a magnolia off at the stem. He started to tug petals off, shredding them as he went. He reminded me of a petulant child, frustrated that he never got his way, and willing to take it out on anything, or anyone who didn't have the power to fight back.

"Ryze respected your opinion," I said. "You two seemed to agree on things."

He shredded harder at the mention of Ryze's name. "Ryze is a fool. I would never have let you go to the Autumn Court with Cavan. I would never have you out of my sight. Or my bed."

He tossed the decimated flower aside and turned to me.

"Fortunately, I won't be making that mistake. In case you think they're coming for you, we have wards all over the Spring Court to keep anyone from portalling in from anywhere else, unless they have spring magic. We've also increased patrols along the border, so they won't be getting in that way either. No one will be coming here until Thiron is ready for them."

I shook my head.

"I don't— I won't—" My voice was high with the strain of trying to speak the words that the order kept suppressing. I couldn't tell him I had no intention of sharing his bed. The words wouldn't come.

On the inside, I was screaming them. Shouting so loud they should have heard me all across Jorius. I couldn't even growl out loud.

My fingers twitched to scratch his eyes out, but when I tried to curl my hands and step forward, I failed.

He smiled. "Yes, you can, and yes, you will. You were born to give pleasure to alphas. That's what you're for. You are going to give me a lot of it." He gripped my hair and pulled me towards him.

He leaned in and slid his tongue over my lip, tasting my mouth.

I wanted to bite it off, but between the order, and my omega instinct to please him, I couldn't move. Couldn't break away when he kissed me. I couldn't stop myself from kissing him back, even though my stomach turned.

"See?" He pulled back enough to smile smugly. "You want to satisfy me. Don't you?"

I fought with the words, but they slipped out anyway. "Yes, alpha."

I wanted to pick up a chair and smash it into his smug, asshole face. Or better yet, grab a knife and cut off his cock. I'd probably live for about thirty seconds after that, but it would absolutely be worth it.

"You asked me if I'm enjoying this. The answer is yes. I've spent the last two hundred years being powerless. But you—"

He gripped my hair so tight it hurt. "With you I have nothing but power. You'll do exactly what I say when I say. At first because you have to, but then because you *want* to. You'll come to learn that obedience to me will be rewarded. When I lift the order, you'll stay. You'll beg to stay because that will be what you want."

He pressed his forehead to mind. "You'll beg to be on your knees, sucking my cock dry. Beg for me to fill that pussy of yours. And I will. I'll fill you with my cock and my children. Our child will be the heir when I'm High Lord."

He made a pleased sound in the back of his throat, like he had it all thought out and everything was going to work out so perfectly. That he'd break me and make my belly swell with the gods only knew how many baby Fae.

I'd often thought the Fae were slightly out of their minds, but he was worse than the others. Did he really believe I'd turn to him? That I'd willingly have his babies? If he did, he was more delusional than the rest.

"You're looking forward to that day, aren't you?" he asked. He actually kissed my forehead.

No, I'm fucking not.

"Yes, alpha." I was going to throw up on his boots. If there was ever a time to believe in the gods, I had to believe in them now. That they'd find a way for Ryze and the other men to get to me.

If I didn't believe in the gods, I believed in those men. None of them would let anything stop them from reaching me. Whatever they had to do, they'd do it. I had to believe in that. Cling to it with everything I had.

"Good," he said, his tone soothing, laced with triumph. "Because you belong to me now. Every part of you." He ran his spare hand over my hip and up to my breast. He squeezed my flesh, then pinched my nipple hard.

I let out a tiny squeak of pain. At the same time, my body betrayed me by registering pleasure. I struggled to contain my response. If he knew I enjoyed pain, he wouldn't hold back in inflicting it on me.

He chuckled, seemingly oblivious to anything but his own enjoyment in hurting me.

I'd accused Cavan of having a sadistic streak, but with him, it was playful. A tease because he enjoyed pretending I was beaten, and broken.

Wornar, I knew, would get a great deal of pleasure in breaking me for real. He must have hidden that side of him well for Ryze to have any respect for him at all.

I'd almost liked him myself. Zared, I remembered now, was the only one who didn't. Although, the sentiment was more him disliking Fae in general, than disliking Wornar in particular.

Still, it was more than the rest of us saw.

"You're going to be so much fun to play with, omega," he said. "I can't wait to pound my cock into your pussy. Unfortunately, that will have to wait. I have things to attend to first. And you could use a bath. Get yourself cleaned up. Change into some fresh clothes."

He nodded towards a wardrobe placed at one side of the room. "I'll have someone bring food. Don't leave this room. Get some rest if you feel the need.

Otherwise, wait for me to return. Spend your time thinking about the ways you're going to please me. How your pussy is going to be dripping wet for me. How much I'm going to punish your mouth, and your pussy. Your whole body. Every sweet centimetre of it."

He pinched my nipple, harder this time. Hard enough to bring tears to my eyes.

"Make sure to wash his blood off you," he added. "Don't leave any sign of him on any part of your body. Inside or out. Tonight will be a new start for both of us."

"Actually, definitely get some rest. You'll be needing it." He chuckled as though he said something hilarious and not repulsive.

He let me go then and pushed me towards the bathing room.

I would wash all right, but I felt dirtier from his touch than I did from Cavan's blood all over my hand and wrist. How the hells were we all so wrong about him?

I had to try to find a way out of here somehow. Like he said, if anyone could find a way around the order, it was me. The problem was, I was finding it difficult to figure out a way how, and that was making me start to panic.

Whatever happened, I wouldn't let him break

me. I'd find my way through this. He might make me do things I didn't want to do, but I could still be strong. I'd survived this long, I'd keep surviving.

I held myself together until the door closed behind him, then I allowed myself a couple of minutes to cry before pouring myself a bath and slipping under the warm, refreshing water.

3

ZARED

I stood near the doorway, hand hovering over my knife, and stewed.

When Khala's frantic rush of emotion came down the bond, I wanted to go straight to her. I'd insisted, but in typical Fae fucking form, the other two ignored me.

"We need to get to Cavan first," Ryze said. "We can't afford to lose a High Lord. Even with a clear heir, it can take years to settle succession. We don't have years." Those were the words that came out of his mouth. The expression on his face said he wanted to go right to Khala.

I wanted to slap his priorities straight.

"Isn't that exactly what Wornar wants? To distract you while he does the gods knows what to her?" Everyone seemed surprised by Wornar's betrayal. Everyone but me. I hadn't trusted him for half a heartbeat. Not just because he was Fae. No, the fucker always seemed way too nice. In my experience people that smooth were usually faking it.

When I felt Khala's confusion and then fear through the bond I wasn't even slightly surprised, but I was furious. Blindly, murderously furious.

The next time I saw Wornar, he'd better hope he was already dead, because if he wasn't I would kill him. I didn't give a fuck if that messed with the succession of the Spring Court.

I'd more or less come to terms with Tavian, Ryze, Cavan and Vayne touching my woman, but no other fucker got away with it.

"We will get her back," Ryze said definitely. "He only has a couple of minutes' head start on us, and Khala is capable of taking care of herself." He was trying to look like he wasn't as worried about her as I was, but he wasn't fooling anyone.

Vayne and I gave him the same flat as shit, disbelieving look.

Vayne shook his head. "You better be right." In spite of having to work with Cavan, the commander of the Winter Court army, clearly still didn't trust him either. Trust was as thin on the ground right now as snow.

"I'm always right," Ryze said, his expression his usual smug arrogance. Prick.

"Except when you're not," I told him.

"He better be right about this, or we won't let him forget it," Tavian said.

He stood near the other side of the door, his eyes on the street. He hadn't questioned Ryze, but he was clearly as antsy as I was. I didn't want to admit it to myself, but it was only his presence which kept me from completely losing my mind.

In spite of his obvious anxiety, he was keeping more or less calm. He probably wanted to slice a bunch of throats open to let off steam.

Ryze had muttered something about not getting any respect, and opened a portal to the Autumn Court.

That was an hour ago. He, Vayne and a healer were still crouched beside Cavan, who finally had some colour back in his face. He was pale, and covered in so much blood when we arrived, I'd thought he was dead already.

As Fae went, he was tolerable, but if it was too late for him then we could go straight after Khala.

When Ryze detected a heartbeat, he ordered me

to stay near the door and stop anyone from entering. I was going to tell him I didn't take orders from him, but Vayne nodded.

Since I'd apparently been recruited into the Winter Court army, I *did* take orders from Vayne.

So I stood, guarded the door with Tavian, and waited.

Waited while Wornar and Khala were so far away. The bond was stretched thin, like my patience. She seemed unhurt, but also unhappy. Angry. Scared. Alone.

For the first time in my life, I wished I was Fae and had magic to make a portal of my own. I would have left these assholes behind and gone after her myself.

The reminder I was a powerless human didn't do much for my state of mind. Especially when the staff from the inn kept giving me looks like I was tomorrow's breakfast. Literally.

I bared my teeth at one who got too close, but ignored them after that. Let them think I was a feral animal, as long as they stayed the hells away.

"Can you stand?" Ryze was asking Cavan.

"Only if you give me some room," Cavan replied.

Apparently being stabbed hadn't improved his personality. Nor had the fact Ryze seemed to have saved his life by freezing the area around the knife and pulling it free. His magic had cauterised the wound and stopped it from bleeding. That in turn gave the healer enough time to arrive and do whatever she did to close it completely.

Apart from the blood all over his clothes, no one would know he had a knife embedded between his ribs only minutes ago. Put there by Khala on Wornar's orders.

Gods, I knew how badly she must be feeling about that. She would have felt worse if he'd died. For that reason alone, this side quest to save Cavan might be worthwhile.

If we didn't, it would gnaw at her for the rest of her life, her choice or not.

I hated the fact any alpha could manipulate her. Loathed it every bit as much as she did. No one should have that kind of control over my woman. No one.

Fucking alphas.

I hated that I wasn't one. If I was, we could have run away and lived our lives away from all of the Fae.

I wouldn't dwell on the fact she might not have run away with me at all. For some reason, she seemed to genuinely care about these men. They cared about her too, but not as much as I did. None of them knew her as well as me. She and I were friends when she was still a Silent Maiden. When I used to tease her by pretending I didn't understand every single one of her hand symbols, including all the nuances she probably wasn't even aware of throwing in. The little flicks of her fingers or her wrists that showed more irritation, or humour than the symbols themselves allowed for.

Ryze and Vayne stood and gave Cavan room to stand on wobbly legs. He held his hands out to the sides until he regained his balance and nodded.

"We need to go after Khala." He teased the edges of his shirt apart and frowned at the fading stab wound. The skin was still puckered and red, but even as we watched, it became paler and smooth.

"That's the most sensible thing anyone said all day," I grumbled.

So sensible I could *almost* forgive feeling him fuck Khala through the bond last night. And yesterday. He hadn't taken long to make his move once they were alone.

Like Wornar's betrayal, that wasn't a surprise either. He was as hot for her as the rest of us. Of course he'd take advantage of the time they had together. It's something we all would have done, given the chance. It was something I'd done when-ever I could. The woman was irresistible.

Tavian murmured his agreement. He pulled out his knife and was using it to clean under his nails. His body language suggested he'd throw it in half a heartbeat, just because he could. That and the other eight or nine he had on him.

Cavan stared at me for a moment, then at Ryze. "Why are you here? Wornar has the key and her. You should have gone after them first."

"That's what I told them," I said. "They seemed to think you were more important."

Tavian grunted under his breath.

"We never said he was more important," Ryze argued. "Just that—" He shook his head. "We can stand here and argue or we can go after them."

I gestured toward the door and almost struck my hand on High Lord Harel's chest as he stomped into the inn.

I dropped my hand and moved away. Not because I was intimidated, not a chance. No, I moved because he was an even bigger asshole than most Fae. The best place to be when he was in a room was on the other side of it. Or better yet, in a different room.

He looked at me like I was the worst kind of

vermin he'd ever seen, and walked past me, chin high like he was king of the gods. Since the gods didn't have a king, he was shit out of luck with that assumption.

"I shouldn't be surprised to find you all here, and in each other's company," he drawled. "Did you think I wouldn't hear of it?"

Tavian watched him through narrowed eyes. His fingernail cleaning paused. I could almost see him calculating the distance and how hard he'd have to throw to embed the knife in Harel's brain. He even gripped the hilt of the knife and checked the balance, right before he slipped it up his sleeve instead.

"I figured you would, sooner or later, Harel," Ryze said. "We were just leaving." He started to step towards the door, but the way was barred by several guards in deep red and gold uniforms.

"Or we could stay a bit longer. I didn't realise you enjoyed our company that much." Ryze smiled sarcastically, but there was worry in his eyes. Not for the guards or Harel, but for Khala.

When this was over and she was safe, I was going to enjoy telling him I told you so, in as many different ways as I could. Just because I was human didn't mean I was wrong. And I was right about that.

Even if Cavan died. All right, I might have regretted his loss almost as much as Khala would. He was part of our pack. His magic might be needed to get her back.

Harel smirked at Ryze, then looked Cavan up and down. "It looks like someone tried to save me the trouble of having you executed for stealing my key. Did you think I wouldn't know? That I'd see the replacement you put in its place and not know it for what it was?"

Cavan shrugged unapologetically. "We only needed to fool you long enough to get out of the Autumn Court. I didn't anticipate taking quite this long."

"From the report I heard, it was your pretty, broken omega who did this." For some reason, Harel seemed to find that amusing.

"If you know that, then you also know I don't have the key anymore," Cavan said wearily. "It went with her."

"It would have gone with Wornar," Harel corrected. "As it happens, it didn't go anywhere. I haven't kept the real key to Nallis in the side of my throne for years. Not since I exiled Illaria. I expected, at some point, she'd give that information to someone."

Ryze's laughter broke the momentary silence. "I don't mind being outsmarted by you, if it means outsmarting someone who betrayed me. Who betrayed all of us."

"It won't matter if he plans on destroying, or hiding the key. He'll be destroying a fake." Cavan pressed a finger to his lower lip. The side of his mouth twitched upward.

"It matters because we still have access to it," Ryze said. "Admittedly, I'd like to be there to see him try to use it and fail." He sighed. "You can't have everything, I suppose."

"You can't have the key either," Harel said. "I'm sure I didn't give you the impression I intended to give it to you."

"After the effort we went to, to try to get it from you, do you really think we'd do that for nothing?" Ryze asked rhetorically. "I know you don't believe in the other courts, but what if we're right and not following through means dooming us all? Are you really willing to take the chance?"

"Does any of this matter right now?" I asked. "We need to go after Khala."

"If you can just give us the key—" Cavan started.

"The key stays in the Autumn Court," Harel said firmly. "I've wasted enough of my time here. You

have two minutes to make a portal and get the fuck
out of my court. If you don't, I will have you appre-
hended and executed. With any luck, this nonsense
will end there."

"We'll go," Ryze said after a couple of moments'
pause. "But we can assure you, this will not end here.
You can bury your head in a pile of leaves as much
as you like, but Jorius is under threat. Pretending it's
not won't make it go away."

"One and a half minutes," Harel said impatiently.

Ryze rolled his eyes and ushered all of us
towards the door. "Your hospitality is worse than
Cavan's. No offence, Cavan."

"Offence   taken,"   Cavan   said   dryly.   "Don't
compare me to Harel."

I decided they were all as bad as each other, but
kept my mouth shut and hurried into the morning
sunshine.

Judging by the expression on Tavian's face, he
was thinking much the same as me. He was unimpressed by the High Lords bickering with each other.
More was at stake than their fragile fucking egos

Ryze waved a few people aside until a space in
the middle of the wide plaza was empty.

Apparently opening a portal too close to people
was dangerous or something. Right now, I didn't give

a shit. I wanted to be gone from here. I wanted to hold Khala and punch the crap out of Wornar. Not necessarily in that order. I'd play that by ear.

Ryze frowned, but eventually had a portal open and waved us through.

I didn't much care for the expression on his face as he did it. Enough was wrong right now. What the crap *else* was happening? We needed to focus our attention on getting Khala back.

I followed Vayne and Cavan through the portal, with Ryze and Tavian right behind me. Ryze closed the portal the moment he stepped out.

The very same moment Vayne turned around to stare at him. "What the hells?"

"This isn't the Spring Court," Cavan added.

"No, it definitely isn't." Tavian's knife was in his hand again. As long as he didn't plan to use it on me, and he acted quickly, I didn't give a shit who he used it on. We'd wasted more than enough time already.

We were standing in a field, a few metres from a stand of trees. Somewhere in the distance I heard what sounded like a waterfall. Or rushing water of some kind. Nothing gave me any indication what court we were in. We could have been back in Fraxius, for all I knew.

"Where the fuck are we?" I demanded.

"In the Winter Court," Ryze said. "On the border. I tried opening a portal to the Spring Court, but it wouldn't let me. They've put wards around the entire court."

"Fuck," Vayne said under his breath.

I looked from one to the other. "What does that mean?"

"It means," Ryze said slowly, "Thiron was planning for a while to keep us out. It also means we can't get to the capital through a portal."

"So we walk." I raised my hands and dropped them back to my sides. Whatever it took to get to her.

"Even without dodging border patrols, it will take us a few days to walk to Lanrial from any point along the border." Ryze kicked a rock in frustration.

I gaped at him. "There has to be another way."

"Can you fly? Because unless you can, there is no other way." Ryze looked ready to tear off heads. He could get in line behind me.

"Now would be a really good time for dragons to exist." Vayne looked as stabby as the rest of us.

"Griffins exist," Tavian said.

"Would you happen to have one in your pocket?" Ryze asked him. "Because if you don't, then they're as useful to us as dragons."

"If one fit in my pocket, it would be as useless as shit," Tavian said. "Unless you have magic to make it big enough for us to sit on its back."

"None of this talking is getting us to the Spring Court any faster," I said, irritated with their banter.

"What would?" Tavian asked. He directed the question to Cavan and Ryze.

It was Vayne who responded. "If we are where I think we are, there's a river not far from here. We could borrow a boat. That would save at least half a day's walking."

"More than that, if Ryze and I can work together and make a breeze to move us along faster," Cavan said.

"By borrow, do you mean steal?" I asked.

"Do you have a problem with us stealing?" Ryze asked. He seemed genuinely curious.

"Fuck no," I replied. "Whatever gets us to her faster." There was nothing I wouldn't do right now to achieve that. *Nothing.*

"Good. Let's go then." Ryze led the way through the trees.

4

ZARED

"She'll be all right," Tavian said as we walked as quickly as we could through the late morning. "She's tough and brave and smarter than all of us put together. Which is saying something, because we're all pretty smart."

"Says you," Vayne said over his shoulder.

"We're all smart except Vayne," Tavian teased.

Vayne stuck up his middle finger behind his back without glancing back at us.

Tavian managed half a smile which was half more than I did.

"If he touches a hair on her head..." I wasn't even sure which he I meant. It didn't matter. Wornar, Thiron, whoever. I'd cut off their balls and jam them down their throat.

"We can either take turns making him suffer, or we can do it at the same time," Tavian said. "I don't care which it is."

"You can get in line," Ryze said. "In the meantime, we need to be quiet." He waved us down.

I dropped to a crouch and moved over beside him.

There, nestled between the trees and tall grass, a handful of huts sat beside a river that wound silently through the countryside. It must be fed by the waterfall I'd heard earlier, For now it was a tranquil, but rapid flow.

"Can't you just commandeer a boat?" I asked.

"Firstly, I don't want word of my presence here to get out. Approaching people would potentially do that," he said slowly.

"And secondly, we crossed the border into the Spring Court about ten minutes ago. Even if they aren't looking out for us, we won't be welcome here."

"I thought you and Thiron were friendly?" Cavan asked.

"It's as much a surprise to me as it is to anyone else," Ryze admitted. "I'll be having stern words with Thiron the next time I see him. All of this division is exactly how we *shouldn't* be right now. We spent too many years getting complacent and snarky with each other. This is the result of that."

"Maybe having four separate courts is a bad idea," I pointed out. "Why do you have four when you can have one?"

"Because we'd argue over who was going to be king," Cavan said.

"And then there'd be war," Tavian added.

"Unless everyone agrees I should be king," Ryze said. "I'd be a good Fae king."

"Because you're good at faking it?" Cavan suggested.

Ryze snorted a laugh. "I never fake, but that is a faking good joke."

Vayne groaned. "Now you've started them off on puns. I hope you realise, Ryze won't stop until they're out of his system. That could take hours."

"That's the faking truth," Tavian agreed. He grinned, but it wasn't with as much humour and joy as usual. Dampening his spirits was a challenge at the best of times. Just now, he looked like someone dumped a bucket of snow on his.

"Can you point me in the direction of the capital," I said. "It might be less painful to go there by myself."

"I'll go with you," Vayne agreed. "Anything to get away from the puns."

Ryze patted him on the shoulder. "Some day you might lighten the fake up."

"If you don't stop it, I'm going to get my knife and ram it through your faking eyeball," Vayne growled.

"None of us would stop you," I told him.

"Quiet," Cavan said suddenly.

To the surprise of all of us, we immediately fell silent.

I froze on the spot, listening, while wishing I had Fae hearing. I made out the faint sound of voices, and movement through the trees. A crack of a twig here, rustle of leaves there. Nothing anyone would hear if they weren't paying close attention.

Vayne gestured to the south of us and Ryze nodded.

"We need to get to the village and find a boat," Ryze whispered.

"We need a distraction," Cavan added.

He sighed, but rose and headed in the direction Vayne pointed. He staggered with exaggerated steps until he caught the attention of the border patrol. Apparently being covered in blood was useful once in a while.

Ryze gestured us towards the village, if you could

call it that. It was little more than a handful of small wooden buildings and a dock that jutted out into the river. A couple of small boats were tied to the worn pilings. A larger dock occupied a chunk of the opposite bank, a wide ferry bobbing against it.

Shouting came from behind us, accompanied by a couple of flashes of light. It wasn't until I smelled the smoke that I realised the light was flame.

The acrid smell was followed by heavy footsteps as Cavan ran to catch up.

"I think I got them all," he panted. "Hurry." He looked tired. After losing all that blood, he probably needed to eat and rest.

Like the rest of us, he wasn't going to rest easily until our mate was back with us.

Even then, I might stay awake until the end of time to make sure no one tried to take her from me again.

I tried to ignore the smell of burning meat as I ran to the closest boat and started to untie the rope that held it in place.

"Never mind that," Cavan said. "Get in."

I glanced at him, but nodded and did what he said. I realised why when all of us were in and another flash of flame burned the rope away.

"Don't set the boat on fire," Ryze warned. If I

didn't know better, I'd almost think he was enjoying himself.

"That's what you're here for," Cavan told him. "To make sure I don't." He gave Ryze a smirk.

Ryze gave him one in return.

I moved to sit closer to Tavian while the two High Lords quickly figured out how to combine their magic to make wind.

"Khala could have done it by herself," Tavian whispered. His hand found its way to mine. He gave it a squeeze.

"You really think she'll be all right?" I asked, my voice low so no one could hear the tremble in my tone. "You know these Fae better than I do. Would they hurt her?"

He took a while to respond. "I thought I knew them," he said slowly. "But now I realise I didn't know them at all. Before I met you, I would have said Cavan is an enemy and Wornar is a friend."

"Now?" I absently stroked my thumb across the inside of his wrist.

"Now I trust Cavan almost as much as I trust Ryze, but Wornar... He's an alpha. He got his hands on an omega, possibly for the first time. I can only guess what that might do to him. We seem to have a way of getting under people's skin without meaning to."

He gave me a glance, but didn't smile. He didn't mean Wornar might fall for her. He honestly didn't know whether he'd hurt her or not.

"That thing where alphas order you," I started.

"We can't fight it," he said, his tone and expression hollow. "I can't explain it. If he orders her to do something, she'll do it. No matter what it is. Even if she hates the idea. Even if it hurts her. You only have to see what he made her do to Cavan. You can't think for a moment she wanted to stab him. She'd only do that if she was angry with him, and she wasn't."

"No, she wasn't." I felt that much through the bond. She was horrified at what Wornar made her do. I didn't want to imagine how much worse it might get for her.

However fast Ryze and Cavan made the boat go, it wasn't fast enough.

5

KHALA

*T*he sunset painted the sky with streaks of pink and gold. A woman of middle years brought me a tray of soup and fresh bread.

For a Fae to look as she did, she must have been old. Of course I didn't ask.

I waited until she left and sat down to eat. I didn't waste time worrying that it might be laced with something. If they wanted me dead, they'd kill me. And if they wanted me incapacitated in some way, they'd order me.

So I ate and enjoyed the flavours of the vegetables in the soup and the freshness of the bread.

I could say this about the Spring Court; they knew how to cook.

I was just mopping up the last of my soup when

Wornar slipped in the door. Almost immediately, the food threatened to sour in my belly.

"It looks like I have perfect timing," he said smoothly. "You can speak freely. I'd prefer you to be willing."

I hadn't realised how heavily his orders lay until he lifted them. When they were gone, I felt like I could breathe again.

"If you were here a couple of minutes earlier, I could have dumped my soup on your head," I said with mock sweetness. I probably shouldn't provoke him, but he gave me permission to speak my mind, so I took it.

He laughed. "So feisty." He propped his elbows on the table and leaned towards me. "I would have liked to see you try."

I managed to resist the urge to sit back away from him. "It would have been worth it." Maybe I could singe his face with magic instead.

Before I could even try, he held up a finger and pointed at my face. "No using magic on me. That's an order I won't be lifting. Omega magic is too dangerous to be on the loose."

"I still have a spoon." I held it up as though to stab him with it.

"Terrifying." He snatched the spoon and tossed it

into the bowl with a clatter. "I thought we could have a little fun. A chance for you to get your freedom. If you dare to try." He arched an eyebrow at me.

"I dare if it means getting away from you," I told him. I still felt dirty from his touch. If there was a chance I could escape the Spring Court, I'd take it.

"I was hoping you'd say that." The smile he gave me was dark, brutal. Shivers slid up and down my spine.

What had I gotten myself into? Whatever it was, he wasn't going to make this easy.

"Come with me." He stood and made a portal in front of us.

Wherever we were going, it wasn't far. I saw right through into a forest, where the last rays of the sun gilded the trees. It was beautiful in a chilling kind of way.

Night would fall soon. I had a feeling we'd be out there alone.

"I see you're starting to appreciate what I have in mind," he said. "Step through."

Not because he told me to, but because this might be my chance to flee, I stepped through.

He followed me and closed the portal behind us.

The forest was almost silent, the air cool and still. A lingering scent of lemon and eucalyptus hung in the air, along with the faint smell of roses and lavender.

I wrapped my arms around myself and moved across the forest floor, away from him.

"Where are we?" I asked.

"We're a few kilometres from the border." He leaned back against the trunk of a tree and regarded me through half-lidded eyes.

I wished I had a knife I could use on him right now.

"Why are we here?" I felt for the other men through the bond, but they were even further away now.

"Have you ever been hunting?" He cocked his head at me. He spoke in such a pleasant tone, he could have been asking if I'd ever had chocolate. Or if I'd been in love.

"No, never. It's not really the kind of activity Silent Maidens get up to."

"Seems a shame to miss out on all the fun." He clicked his tongue. "Never mind, we can make up for it tonight."

I swallowed and started to wish I hadn't eaten anything. The soup and bread turned to lead in my stomach.

"What are we hunting?" I asked carefully. I was almost certain I knew the answer to that question.

"We're not hunting," he said easily. He straightened up and lowered his hands to his sides. "*I'm* hunting. I'll give you a couple of minutes head start. If you can make it across the border before I catch you, you can go free."

My shivers turned to cold fear.

"And if you catch me?"

He stepped over to me and leaned in. He smiled as he spoke. "Then I get to keep you. One word of advice. Run."

I didn't stop to think, I turned and fled into the trees.

His laughter followed, mocking, unhurried. Like he was so certain I'd panic and he'd catch me easily.

Don't panic, I told myself. *He wins if you do.* I couldn't run blindly and hope to outrun him. I had to reason clearly. Where exactly was the border?

I wouldn't let myself think about what might happen if he decided to break his word, if I crossed before he caught me and he decided to keep me anyway.

I had to focus on getting across.

The sun was setting, so I knew which way was west.

I pictured the map in my mind. The placement of the four courts. The Spring Court was north of the Winter Court, and west of the Summer Court. If I ran west, I'd run deeper into Spring Court territory.

I veered off towards the east. Running into the deepening shadows.

No doubt that was his plan. He assumed in my fear I'd head for the part of the forest where I could still see where I was going. Logical, given how quickly it became difficult to see much of anything in front of me.

I considered using magic to illuminate the way. If I did that, I might as well stand amongst the trees and shout. Any light would give my location away. The only chance I had was to find my way in the dark.

I slowed, moving quieter. Snapping twigs under my feet would resound like thunder out here. The crack of several behind me said he'd started to follow.

Don't panic, I told myself again. What would Tavian do? He was a trained assassin. He'd slip away and be across the border before Wornar could blink.

I tried to put myself in his mindset. How exactly did an assassin move so quietly? Become one with the trees or something?

I tripped over a root and almost fell to my knees. I managed to save myself at the last moment and staggered on a few steps.

"You smell delicious, sweet omega," Wornar called out behind me. "Like a spring rain on a field abundant with lavender. Good enough to eat and drink."

I shivered and went on moving. Now he mentioned it, I could smell him too. The scent of an alpha mixed with that of fresh grass and that first warm breeze of spring.

I needed to cover my scent. He said I couldn't use magic against him, he didn't say I couldn't use it at all.

I paused for maybe half a minute, winced at the flash before the tree behind me caught fire. For once, the unseasonable warmth worked in my favour. The bark was drier than it might otherwise have been. Flames roared up into the canopy in moments, down to ignite the leaf matter on the ground.

The smoke would help to cover my scent, but the fire spread quickly. I turned from it and fled.

"You'll be punished for that," Wornar called out.

All the more reason to get away.

I glanced over my shoulder to see he'd stopped,

and was using magic to douse the flames. I couldn't see what he was doing, but it seemed effective.

I sent a quick request to the gods that it would be enough to delay him until I reached the border. I didn't try to be quiet now. I ran.

A couple of times I tripped and fell, wincing as my knees scraped, digging into twigs. I immediately pulled myself back to my feet and kept on running.

By now, the sun was little more than a slight blush behind me. Everything in front of me was so dark I was forced to run with my hands up in front of me to keep from slamming face first into a tree.

I glanced back again. The fire was out. The sun was completely gone. The forest was entirely dark and stank heavily of smoke. He might have more difficulty finding me, but I also had no idea where he was. And no way of knowing when I reached safety.

What had he said? A couple of kilometres to the border? How far had I run? Not that far, not yet. Even if I had, I'd run twice that, just to be sure. And then go on running until the sun rose.

I dashed tears off my cheeks. I told myself they were from the smoke, not because I was scared. Not because I thought at any moment now, he'd catch up to me. If I was a human, he would have caught me by now. But I was Fae. I was taller, faster. I could evade him.

"Are you getting tired?" he asked.

Fuck.

There was no way he was as close behind me as he sounded. He couldn't be. I didn't dare to look back and check.

"I'm not," he called out. "I could go all night. And I will, the moment I catch you."

If he was trying to make me run faster, he succeeded. The threat of what he'd do to me gave me renewed energy.

In spite of that, I slowed down. If he couldn't smell me as easily, then I needed to rely on stealth to evade him. Stealth and cunning.

I ducked past a tree and formed a sheet of ice across the forest floor behind me. The moon was starting to rise, but not enough to illuminate it.

Let's see how you deal with that, I thought.

I rose and kept on moving.

After what felt like an eternity, but was probably a minute or two, he gave a short cry of surprise. That was followed by a heavy thump.

When I was at the temple in Ebonfalls, they taught us about the rules of the gods. Things that just were. Rocks can't fall up. If something doesn't have wings, it can't fly. I'd added a couple of others myself, like it's extremely difficult to fit more than two cocks into my pussy at the same time.

I added a new one now. Ice is slippery. Don't try running across it. The thud of his body hitting the forest floor was satisfying as fuck.

"Fucking bitch," Wornar snarled.

Not sorry, I thought. Was it too much to hope he'd broken a leg and couldn't keep after me? Judging by the sound of stomping and the angry smashing of branches, he hadn't broken any bones. Shame.

"I'm going to make you regret doing that," he called out. He was gaining on me again. "When I'm finished with you, you'll beg for my forgiveness."

In your dreams, I thought. What I could use right now was one of those portals in the air, a gift from the other courts, and some magic aimed at him. It was effective in getting rid of Dalyth. Why not Wornar as well?

No portal appeared. I hadn't expected it to. It seemed to follow Hycathe around, not me. That was something I didn't have time to dwell on right now.

I darted through the trees and ducked low as I crossed a section of open grassland. I half waited for him to pounce, exposed as I was for a minute or two.

By the time I dove back into the trees, he seemed further behind somehow. I didn't stop to wonder why until the ground tilted down.

I lost my balance and rolled and slithered all the way down, painfully bumping over rocks and sticks. Finally, I landed with a splash in frigid water.

The shock of the sudden cold made me gasp out loud. I was covered in scrapes and bruises, but as far as I could tell, nothing was broken.

Suppressing a grunt of pain, I forced myself back to my feet. I was standing on the edge of a river. In the starlight, I made out its progress as it flowed past.

"Fuck," I whispered. It was flowing west, straight back into the Spring Court. Of course it was. He must have hoped I'd get caught in the flow and dragged back. Asshole.

I'd never managed to make a bridge like Ryze could, but I grabbed enough magic to make an ice wall. The last time I did it, I almost killed Zared. This time, if anyone behind me got caught in it, I wouldn't spare any sympathy or tears.

The flow of the river was blocked for a couple of metres in either direction, but it wouldn't hold for long. It would overflow right to where I was currently standing in a minute or two.

I sucked in a breath for bravery, then bolted

across the river bed, my feet slipping on mud as I went. Every few steps, I had to pause and yank my foot free. I lost one shoe, then the other, but kept on going.

I managed to reach the other bank and scrambled up, breaking fingernails and skin as I pulled myself free of the mud.

I turned to look back over the river.

Wornar stood looking at the wall. The moon had risen high enough to illuminate him. The admiration on his face. He didn't seem to be breathing as heavily as I was. Perhaps he made a habit of chasing women through the forest.

"Nice trick." He clapped his hands together a couple of times.

"I thought so," I called back. I used a bit of summer magic to help melt the wall and let the river flow back to its bed. I must be close to the border now, and he was on the other side.

His teeth flashed right before he opened a portal and stepped through.

The other end appeared right beside me. I wasn't good at keeping portals open, but I was good at closing them. I grabbed all the magic I could and focused on trying to do just that.

If I could snap it shut at this end, he might get

stuck in there. Or better yet, squashed to death. I was absolutely all right with that.

He growled and staggered back out, before closing it himself and opening another one.

I did the same with this one, teeth gritted, fighting to not only shut it, but push it. Push it where, I didn't know. Just...away.

Something made me glance over to the opposite bank. He'd moved away from the portal and was getting ready to make another one.

I stopped pushing on the portal in front of me, turned away and ran. I considered trying to make my own portal and getting the hells out of here, but if it behaved like they always had in the past, he'd catch me while I was trying to keep it open. I couldn't afford to waste that time.

"Are you having as much fun as I am?" He was on the same side of the river now, but he was dry and still had his boots on.

I had bare feet and wet clothes holding me back. I also had the determination not to let him catch me.

"It's adorable that you think you can make it," he added. "You're close, so close. But not close enough. You might as well give up right now. I know there's a part of you that wants to. A place in your omega heart that wants to surrender to me.

Embrace it. Save your energy for other things. Better things."

Yes, there was a very small part of me that instinctively felt the need to please the alpha in him, but it was small enough to ignore. And overridden with thoughts of Cavan, Ryze, Tavian, Vayne and Zared. Pleasing two alphas, two betas and another omega was much more important to me. My pack. They overrode everything. Everything I was, belonged to them.

I was tiring, but I clung to what Wornar said about being close to the border. Had he expected me to get this far? Maybe he hoped I would, just for the thrill of the chase. From some deluded idea that he could teach me who was in charge here. He wouldn't win. He couldn't. Nothing in me could accept that.

I realised the air smelled different. It was clear of smoke. Instead, it smelled like the honeysuckle and wildflowers of summer. I might have imagined the increase in temperature, and it might just be from exertion. Either way, he was right, I was close.

This wasn't like going from one season to another, it was a sensation... A trickle of magic between each court that formed the border. Something only Fae could feel.

There. I wasn't imagining it. There was something ahead, drawing me closer. Something warm like a nest, but more soothing. More compelling.

Safety.

Just another minute or two. A few dozen handfuls of steps.

I didn't know he was right behind me until he grabbed me. We crashed hard to the ground. The impact drove a sob out of my lungs.

He held me down, his weight on mine. He chuckled in my ear.

"Caught you."

6

KHALA

I writhed and fought, trying to push him off and get away. He was too heavy. His weight pinned me to the ground.

I struggled to scream or shout, but landing heavily winded me. It took me a few moments to regain my breath.

Before I could utter a sound, he spoke.

"Don't make any loud noises. I don't want anyone to disturb our fun."

"Get off me," I hissed.

"I want you to feel something." He grabbed my hand.

I pushed back against him. The last thing I wanted to do was touch his cock.

He pulled my hand forward until the tips of my

fingers tingled. "You feel that? Do you know what that is?"

I wanted to both bask in the magic and draw away from it at the same time.

"The border." I managed to speak in a small, bitter whisper.

"That's exactly what it is," he said triumphantly. "See how close you were. You put up a good fight. I'm genuinely surprised. I thought I'd catch you at the first line of trees. But here you are. Just centimetres away from escape. Another couple of steps and you would have done it. But you didn't. You failed. I won, and now I get to keep you."

I curled my fingers away from the border. "I'll never be yours. Ryze, Cavan and—"

"Didn't reach you in time," Wornar finished for me. "It doesn't matter what they do now. It doesn't matter what *you* do. I don't want to force you to comply. I don't want to break you, but if that's what it takes, so be it. Remember this. It's your choice to make. You can force me to force you, or you can be agreeable."

What sort of choice was that?

"If I have a choice, then I choose neither," I said. "Get off me and let me go."

He clicked his tongue. "I can't do that. We had a

deal. If you reached the border first I would have let you go. Besides, I don't want to. I own you now."

He rolled off me, grabbed my hands and pulled me to my feet. "No running away now."

I couldn't run, couldn't use magic against him and I couldn't shout. I was becoming more and more powerless. Stripped down, layer by layer until I was raw.

I refused to give in to despair. I would find a way out, no matter what it took. I would not let him get the better of me.

"You're a stubborn one, are you?" He cocked his head at me. "I can see you thinking about your next move. This doesn't have to be bad. As Fae go, I'm not the worst of us. I'm not going to beat you, or lock you away."

He slid the tip of his finger down my cheek. "All I'm going to do is fuck you. Is that really so terrible?"

I jerked my face away. "Without my consent it is, yes."

"Then give your consent," he said as though it was the easiest thing in the world. "I don't need it. With a few words, I can make you want me. I can make you do whatever I say. I'd rather you didn't force me to do that. Whether I have to or not, is up to you."

He made it sound like he was the victim. That if he took me with force, it would be entirely my fault for making him do it.

"I will never voluntarily fuck you." My voice wavered, betraying the depths of my emotions. The cold fear that started to settle on me.

He shrugged. "So be it." He made a portal beside us and grabbed my wrist to push me through. "Go and have a bath. You smell like smoke and dirt."

I wished I'd incinerated him. So much more than that, I wished I'd made it those handful of steps. To be so fucking close...

"Wait," he said before I started towards the bathing room. "Take your clothes off here. I want to see what I'm getting when you're clean."

The order settled on me, like an executioner's sword. Sharp, heavy and final.

I'd never hated anyone more than I hated him right now. I was a puppet, made to dance on his strings. A puppet who wanted to stab him in the eyeball with a fork.

Tears slid down my cheeks. I gritted my teeth. My body moved beyond my control. I slipped out of my pants and pulled off my shirt.

I dropped them on the floor and looked back at

him with resentment, his face blurry through the haze of tears.

His eyes travelled up and down my bare body. The front of his pants tented. For a while, I thought he might not bother to wait until I was clean.

My whole body trembled. Without touching me he made me feel violated. Dirty. Beyond dirty, filthy.

He nodded. "Go and get clean. I'll be back in a few minutes."

"Take a year if you have to." At least I still had my sassy mouth. Maybe I shouldn't provoke him, but I couldn't see how any of this could get much worse than it already was. If I was lucky, he might get furious enough to kill me.

A flash of anger crossed his face, but it was gone before I could blink. His customary smile was back.

"I could take a year," he said slowly. "It might be interesting to see the effect of the anticipation on you, dear omega. Wondering exactly when I'd return and what I might do when I get back. At some point, you'd become complacent. That would be the exact moment I reappeared. Fortunately, I have no interest in clinging to the anticipation any longer than necessary. Blue balls are much less fun as they sound."

He cupped a hand around his erection, then smiled and left the room.

I swallowed hard and headed into the bathing room to start the bath. Like in the Winter Court, the Spring Court had running hot water, which still fascinated me in spite of my present situation. It was a luxury humans didn't have.

I filled the bath to the top and stepped into the slightly too hot water. It enveloped my skin like a wet embrace, wrapping around me and washing away everything, at least for now.

While I was under there, I could pretend this was all there was in the world. That I wasn't being held against my will by a Fae man who intended to force himself on me. Who seemed to be looking forward to doing that.

It was all I could do to hold myself together and not duck under the water and stay there. That would solve one problem, but it would create too many more. Not the least of which was the potential Ryze and Cavan might go to war with the Spring Court over me.

They still might, but without doubt they would if I was dead. They needed to focus their attention on the other courts and dealing with them. Not worrying about me.

They were, though. I sensed that through the

bond with the four of them. I doubted Cavan was any less worried and determined to reach me.

Right now, they felt so far away. Too far. What were they doing? They didn't seem to be fighting with each other. That was a bonus. They all seemed tense. If I had to decide who was the most strung out, I couldn't. Vayne and Zared were the usual simmering pots of anger waiting to boil over. Ryze was cold, determined fury.

I wouldn't like to be on the receiving end of any of their ire.

I sent them thoughts that I was all right, but I wasn't sure how convincing I was. I certainly didn't convince myself. I was terrified of what might happen tonight. And tomorrow night. And the gods only knew how many nights after that.

I tried not to think about it, but it dominated my thoughts. Of course it did. What else did I have to think about? The idea of being violated enveloped me tighter than the water.

This was exactly what Wornar wanted. It wasn't enough that I knew what he was going to do to me. He wanted me to think about it, to be scared, terrified of the moment he'd step back into the room.

I washed quickly and dried myself off before dressing in clean clothes I found in the wardrobe.

Soft pants in pale blue, and a short-sleeved blouse that barely covered my breasts. The fabric moulded around them, leaving little to the imagination.

I stepped into a section of the room out of sight of the balcony and rubbed my temples for a moment.

If I didn't at least try, I'd never know if I could make a portal here. I knew I could make one, I'd done it before. Then, they hadn't stayed open. But I hadn't been desperate before.

When Ryze tried to teach me, I was angry with him. Not receptive to everything he was trying to tell me. I was angry he'd lied to me. That he hadn't told me there was a chance I'd transform into a Fae. All he told me was that I would go into heat and I'd need him and want him.

It seemed to me as if every part of being an omega meant surrendering my choices. I'd liked him before my heat, but he hadn't presented me with a ton of other alphas to choose from. Or any, in fact. I'd fucked him because my body needed me to. Not because I'd been able to make any conscious decision.

I wasn't only angry because he lied. I was angry because of that too; my lack of choice.

I wasn't angry with him anymore. Now I could

calmly, rationally think about what he told me about forming a portal and keeping it open.

I had no choice. I *had* to get it to work. Wornar thought we had some kind of deal where he got to do whatever he wanted to me because I didn't run fast enough.

As far as I was concerned, we had no such deal. Even if we did, keeping me didn't necessarily mean he got to touch me. He could lock me away in this room forever. As long as he gave me books, it might be a tolerable life. Certainly better than being violated.

I drew together winter and summer magic. If I had no luck with one, maybe I would have luck with the other, or with both. If I did it right, I might convince the magic it was spring magic. Magic wasn't alive, so how hard would it be to trick it?

Gods, please let it be easy.

The air quivered in front of me, like I was looking through a cloud of smoke. A chair in the corner danced and writhed on the other side of the wall of magic.

I ignored it and focused on opening a portal to the first place I could think of. My bedroom in the Winter Court. It was a place of confused and conflicting memories, but also safety.

It was the place where I learned I was part Fae. Where I first discovered that my mother used to be involved with Cavan, before she ran off and married my father. It was a place where Tavian and I spent hours curled up together, talking and touching.

Best of all, it was anywhere but here.

I couldn't see all the way into my room, the portal was too long. The walls were made of what looked like a combination of ice and fire. Crystalline, but at the same time glowing faintly red. I didn't care what it looked like, as long as it got me out of here.

I took a step towards the portal, my heart racing. So far, it was staying open. At any moment now, it might snap shut.

I held my breath and took another step.

A hand clamped around my throat from behind.

"What did I say about not running away?"

A blink later, the portal was gone. And my hope with it.

** $\mathcal{W}$ arning** This chapter contains sexual assault. It's contained within this chapter and only vaguely referenced beyond this point. If you're uncomfortable, you can skip this chapter and not miss out on elements of the story.

"You needn't have bothered to get dressed again," he said. He slid his other hand to the front of my shirt and grabbed my breast. He pinched my nipple between his fingers. "I've been giving this a lot of thought."

"You've decided to let me go." I knew that wasn't what he was saying at all.

He chuckled near my ear. "No, dear omega. I've been deciding whether or not to let you fight me. You will fight me if I let you, won't you?"

"Yes." I tried to jerk myself out of his grip.

He pinched harder. "I thought you might." He slid his hand out of my blouse, grabbed the front and tore it down the middle.

"Listen carefully, little omega. You won't fight me. You'll do exactly what I tell you to do. You want to please me. You want me to fuck you more than you've ever wanted anyone in your entire life. You're going to enjoy every moment of it. When I tell you to, you're going to come for me, and it will be the best orgasm you ever had. Not just tonight, but whenever I want you. You'll be willing and compliant. Eager. Dripping."

Every word he said was another layer on top of an order that was as twisted as fuck. My body immediately throbbed for him. I wanted, needed, him to touch me everywhere. I wanted to spread my legs wide and take him inside me.

And I hated myself for it. The need to scream and cry was pushed into the back of my mind, overpowered by lust.

"Undress yourself, then undress me."

I couldn't stop myself from turning around to face him while stripping quickly. I all but tore the clothes off him, revealing a toned, muscular physique and thick, erect cock. I was trembling again, but this time with the need to feel him fill me.

"Isn't this much more fun?" He looked so smug.

I wanted to punch him in the face.

I managed to whisper, "Please, don't," before he led me over to the bed and laid me down on my back.

He ignored me and parted my thighs with his hands. He slid his hand up one leg and slipped two fingers straight inside my pussy.

"You say don't, but your pussy is dripping wet for me. I think, secretly, you want this as much as I do." He slid in another finger and started to pound me with his hand.

Tears trickled down my cheeks while my body betrayed me by bucking and moving my hips until my clit found the heel of his hand.

"See? In the end, all omegas are whores. All you want is to be fucked. It's what you live for." He ground his hand into my clit, rubbing firmly until I was on the verge of coming. "You're enjoying this, aren't you?"

I wanted to tell him to fuck off, but the only thing that came out of my mouth with the words, "Yes, alpha."

I didn't know what I hated more right now: his ability to control me, him, or myself. My body wasn't my own anymore. As long as I was stuck here with him, I'd never be able to do anything except what he told me to do.

I should have sunk under that bathwater while I could. Any of the seven hells would be better than this.

"Come for me, omega whore," he ordered.

I came hard and fast, rocking and crying out as the world shattered and my body betrayed me even more completely than it already had.

I was barely down when he pulled his fingers out of me, rolled me over and pulled me onto my hands and knees.

"Tell me you want me inside you," he ordered.

No no no. Gods no.

My lips moved and the words came out anyway. "I want you inside me."

Not as much as I want to die right now.

He slipped a hand between us to position himself, then pushed himself deep inside my body.

I couldn't contain a sob, even when it turned into

a moan of pleasure. I hated how good he felt inside me. How full I was. I hated that I could have stayed like that for hours. I hated how good it felt when he started to pound into me over and over with even, firm strokes.

I wanted it to stop and I wanted it to go on forever.

He grabbed my breasts and kneaded them while thrusting.

"You feel good, omega whore. Worth all the waiting. Worth all the preparation. If Ryze and Cavan ever reach Lanrial alive, you'll tell them you want to stay with me. And you'll mean every word of it. If they come. I'm sure by now they have realised all the effort isn't worth it for one omega slut. They'll go back to the usual petty squabbles and we'll get on with our lives. We'll raise the child I'm about to put into your belly. You'll spend the rest of your life adoring me, even if I have to tell you to do it. I'd prefer it if you turned to me, but it doesn't much matter. I don't want you for your companionship, just your body and your womb. Both of those are mine now."

He thrust harder several more times, then stilled as he came inside me.

I screwed my eyes shut and tried to block out the

noise of him and his orgasm. He could make me say I wanted and do things I didn't. He might make me feel things I didn't want to say. But he couldn't change the fact that, at my core, I hated him.

He slumped and panted over my back for a couple of minutes before pulling out of me and flopping down on his back on the mattress.

He looked over at me and smiled at the expression on my face. "Conflicted? That's perfect. I don't care what you want as long as you do what I say. You know why? Because it's an alpha's job to have power over his omega. And your job to obey. I'm sure Ryze has told you something ridiculous like he's supposed to cater to your every need. On the contrary, you're here to take care of mine. Now, get comfortable. I have things to do, but I'll be back later."

He patted me on the ass, then rolled off the bed and pulled his clothes back on.

It wasn't until the door clicked shut behind him that I scrambled off the bed and refilled the bath. I needed to scrub every centimetre of myself clean. To rid myself of his touch. By the time I got into the bath, it was hot as in the first one. Hotter.

My skin turned red the moment I was immersed. I grabbed a brush and started to scrub myself everywhere. When I was done cleaning the outside, I still needed to clean the inside too.

He said I couldn't use magic on him, but he didn't say I couldn't use it on myself.

I focused my thoughts on everywhere between my pussy and my womb. I scoured myself inside with magic so hot I thought I might incinerate myself. I didn't care.

Everywhere his seed might be, I scrubbed. There was no way it could take hold inside me. No way a child that belonged to him could grow inside my body.

In the back of my mind, I understood this might stop me from ever having children, but I didn't care. *Couldn't* care.

I wanted, needed every drop of him gone from me. If this was what I had to do every time he touched me, I would.

I lay back, sank under the water until only my mouth and nose weren't submerged.

I tried to sink a little deeper, but I couldn't bring myself to do it. If I did that, then he won. He got the satisfaction of forcing me to the point where I didn't want to live. I wasn't there yet.

I would *not* let him push me there. No matter what he did, or made me do, I couldn't let him reach every part of me. I could not, would not let him break me.

If I had to endure him using my body every day for the rest of my life, he would *not break me.*

I promised myself that. If he ordered me to rip my own soul in two, I wouldn't let him. Even if all that was left to fight was a small part of me in the back of my mind, I would stand against him.

He would never completely win.

I dragged myself out of the bath for a second time, dried and dressed, and slipped under the covers to curl up into the smallest possible ball.

I forced a wall between me and my three bonds and let the tears come.

I didn't know how long I sobbed. Maybe minutes. Maybe hours. I hated myself again for showing this much weakness, even though I was the only one here to see it.

I had to be stronger than this. I had to be harder than stone. Harder than diamonds. I couldn't afford to be fragile or brittle. I couldn't let anyone put a toe past my walls. Not ever again. Even half a toe would make me vulnerable, and I was done being vulnerable. I was Khala. I was tough.

I told myself that over and over while I sobbed.

I ignored Ryze's attempt to push through my walls and reach me. I shoved him back out.

If I could break the bonds right now, I would. What was the use of them when they couldn't help me when I needed them? Surely there was a way for the men to reach me, even with the wards in place? Had they tried hard enough to get to me?

On the other end, all I'd felt was concern and determination, not battling and struggling to break through into the Spring Court. What use was their worry while I was in here having Wornar force himself on me?

The bonds were useless. All they did was make me vulnerable, because the men on the other end knew what happened to me. They knew what I went through, and they couldn't do a thing. Not one thing. They couldn't stop it, or make it go away. They couldn't give me a place to hide while it happened.

No, all they could do was fucking sympathise. Their fucking sympathy was no fucking use to me. None at all.

Those thoughts made me hate myself even more. They were worried because of me. They shouldn't be.

Wornar and Harel were right, I was nothing more than an insignificant omega whore. My pack should be finding a way to stop the other courts from destroying the seasonal courts. Not wasting time on me. On someone who couldn't even control her own body. Someone who, even now, ached to have Wornar's cock deep inside me again. Who wanted his hands and mouth on my pussy. If he walked into the room right now, I'd spread my legs for him and let him sink deep into me. I'd let him do it again and again and again. Until my body was raw.

I was made for fucking. Why else would the alpha-order exist? Whether the gods had a sense of humour and created omegas for shits and giggles, or not, this was how we were. We were made to be compliant, obedient, willing.

Even when we wanted to be none of those things.

If the gods had a sense of humour, it was the most fucked up thing in the world.

I added the gods to the ever growing list of things I hated right now.

None of those things I hated as much as I hated myself.

8

ZARED

"We need to hurry the fuck up."

How the hells could any of the others stay so calm? I wanted to burn the whole fucking world down right now. Before Khala shut us out, I felt exactly what that asshole did to her.

If he was in front of me right now, I'd tear him into a million pieces. Bad enough that he touched her at all. The whole omega-alpha thing was screwy without being abused.

Without *her* being abused.

Fuck, I wanted to choke that asshole with my bare hands.

"Don't you think we'd go faster if we could?" Cavan whispered.

He gestured at me to keep my head down so I

wouldn't be seen by the passing patrol. They were far enough away they wouldn't hear us whisper, but they'd see us if we moved excessively.

They were the third border patrol we'd seen this morning and the sun was barely a hand span high in the sky.

I glared at him, but looked away.

This was his fault. If he hadn't insisted she go to the Autumn Court in the first place, she wouldn't have been there for Wornar to take. All of that was for nothing, since we didn't have the fucking key anyway. Everything she was going through, was for *nothing*.

If it wouldn't waste time, I might rip him apart too. I still might, later.

A hand touched my shoulder. I didn't have to look to know it was Tavian.

"Fighting amongst ourselves isn't going to help her," he said softly.

The two of us and Ryze felt the same thing from her, but it seemed to hit Tavian almost as hard as it hit me.

In spite of his apparent love of killing people, the Master of Assassins had a sensitive side. And, given he was also an omega, the same thing might have happened to him. Had it happened in the past?

That was a question I couldn't bring myself to ask. Not in front of the other men. It was something best kept for a quiet conversation, when and if he was ready to share. If the expression on his face was any indication, he'd at best been in a similar situation.

"Hiding in the bushes doesn't seem to be helping much either," I said. "Can't we just... I don't know."

"Go home and come back with an army?" Ryze suggested. When I turned to look at him, he gave me a wry look. "Don't worry, I've considered it. The five of us have a better chance of getting in and out quickly, and with minimal loss of life. On both sides."

He must have seen what I was about to say. I didn't give a shit about loss of life from anyone belonging to the Spring Court. If they supported Wornar, then they were the enemy. They deserved to be smashed to pieces by the combined armies of the Winter and Summer Courts.

"I hate to say that Ryze is right," Vayne said, "but in this case, he is. It would take too long to mobilise our army and transport everyone here. Besides, the five of us make up a pretty fucking good army."

"I disagree," Tavian said. "I have a better idea."

"I'm coming with you," I said once he told us. "I

know how to keep quiet." He'd have to tie me down or kill me to keep me from following. He might as well let me accompany him.

He wanted to tell me no, that was obvious from the expression on his face, but finally he nodded. "Fine, but if I tell you to do something, don't argue. This is what I do and I'm good at it. Listen to me and we should be all right. If I tell you to stay behind somewhere, you do it. Agreed?"

I considered for a moment, then nodded. "Whatever it takes."

Ryze rubbed his chin. "I don't like it, but I think it's the only way. We'll be ready for your signal." He nodded to Cavan and Vayne and rose. They headed off east.

After several minutes, Tavian gestured to me and started off to the north.

"You're about to get a crash course in assassin skills. Personally, I think everyone should have them. You never know when the ability to sneak in and out of places will come in handy."

"I get the impression you do that often," I told him.

He gave me a broad smile over his shoulder. "Quite often," he agreed. "Wouldn't want my skills to get rusty."

"Who taught you?" I asked as we slipped through the tall grass and into the shelter of a thicket of trees.

"I was apprenticed to the last Master of Assassins," he said. "I wanted to join the regular army, but he saw something in me and took me under his wing. He taught me how to be silent when it mattered, and told me I could get paid to kill people. He was right, it was the perfect job for me. I would have hated peacetime as a soldier anyway. The constant training is all very well, but it's pretend."

"You prefer real killing?" I asked.

"Only people who deserve it," he said, his tone dark. He didn't try to suppress the undercurrent of violence. It gave me the shivers while at the same time making my cock twitch. He was charming and dangerous, and it would be easy for me to fall for him as hard as I had for Khala.

"I can think of a few of those right now."

"Me too. We can argue later over who is going to kill Wornar. And whether we do it quickly or slowly."

"I don't care how fast it is," I said. "As long as he can't touch her ever again."

Tavian stopped and turned to put a hand on my bicep. "We will get to her. He will pay for what he did."

"I know, but how many more times will he do it before we get there?" She shut us out so firmly, I didn't know if it was happening right now. All I knew was she was alive.

Literally nothing else. All this not knowing was ripping my heart straight out of my chest.

Tavian shook his head. "I don't know. Once is too many. But we need to keep our heads for her sake. If we get caught and killed, it won't help her. The most important part of assassin training is learning how to turn your anger into something productive. Focus on what we'll do when we find her, and what it takes to do that. Don't let your hatred and anger make you do something to jeopardise her. All right?"

I closed my eyes for a moment, then nodded. "I'll try."

"It's okay to think vengeful thoughts, just not rash, angry ones," he said. "She's locked us out right now, that doesn't mean she's going to continue to do that. She needs calm thoughts on the end of the bond. If she reaches out, *when* she reaches out, she'll need reassurance. Can you do that?"

"I can," I said firmly. He was right. Khala didn't need my emotions in turmoil. For all I knew, she felt everything flowing from us to her.

I immediately regretted my fury. What if I made

things worse for her? I might be as bad as Wornar if I did that.

"I know you can." Tavian gave me a quick kiss on the mouth. "You're one of the most amazing people I know. Now— we should keep going. We're about half a day from Lanrial. If we hurry, we can be there by nightfall. By the time the sun rises again, we'll be back home. All of us safe and sound."

My lips tingled where his touched mine, but I didn't have time to think about that right now. Khala was what mattered, not whatever was growing between me and Tave. That was something we could deal with later.

"I like the sound of that."

His whole body went stiff. He pulled me into a crouch beside him.

I didn't question him, I dropped and listened.

He leaned over to whisper in my ear. "Stay here. I'll be two minutes." He crept off silently.

It couldn't have been more than half a minute later when a short cry was followed by a soft thud. Another came half a minute after that. Someone shouted, but it was cut off as quickly as the first two.

A few seconds later, Tavian reappeared. He was wiping blood off a knife with a piece of what looked like someone's shirt. He grinned at my questioning look.

"Border patrol. By the time anyone finds them, we'll be long gone." He slipped his knife away and waved for me to follow him through the trees.

We stepped silently past three Fae men, each with their throats sliced open.

I should probably find it disturbing how pleased Tavian looked with himself. I didn't. I actually found it hotter than a sane man probably should. He'd killed them all so quickly and efficiently, before any got the chance to raise any kind of alarm.

"Can you teach me how to do that?" I asked.

"Of course," he agreed. "There's a fourth man maybe twenty metres from where we are. As far as I can tell, he's alone. He's all yours." He gestured ahead of us.

I hadn't known anyone was there until he mentioned it. Now he had, I listened and looked. At first, I thought he was wrong, but then I heard the snap of a twig. They had no reason to try to keep silent. That worked to my advantage.

I slipped out a knife and crept through the trees, moving carefully around a fallen log or anything else that might make noise if I stepped on it.

I peered around a wide trunk. A Fae man with

red-gold hair that hung down his back faced away from me.

He was slightly taller, but I had the advantage of him not knowing I was there. I'd have to be quick and careful. I didn't have the hearing or reflexes of a Fae. I had to rely on my human senses and skills, and the training I got at the Temple and in the Winter Court.

I bent down to pick up a rock that lay at the base of a tree. I pulled my arm back and threw it as hard as I could.

When the man turned towards the sound, I rushed out of the trees and drove my knife into the side of his neck.

His eyes widened. He stared at me before he started to fall. I grabbed him, supported his weight, before lowering him silently to the forest floor.

I slid my knife out of his neck and watched the blood flow and pump out onto the ground. He let out a last, ragged breath, then fell still.

It wasn't a quick, clean kill like Tave's, but he was just as dead.

"Nice work." Tavian was leaning against the trunk of a tree, his arms crossed over his chest. He nodded his approval, then pushed himself off the trunk and stepped over.

"I'm sure he won't mind if you take his knife and his sword. He doesn't have any use for either of them anymore. His sword is better than the one you're carrying. The steel one anyway." He grinned.

I snorted softly and drew the sword out of its sheath. The blade was long, slender and sharp. The hilt was a perfect fit for my hand, although the design was nothing fancy.

I didn't need fancy, I needed deadly. Made by a master.

In comparison, mine was made for the Temple, with lower quality steel, and a less than honed skill by a human swordsmith.

"It will do," I said casually, as though the weapon in my hand wasn't considerably superior to the one on my back. I swapped them over, leaving mine in the Fae man's sheath.

"Now you have two good quality swords." Tave grinned.

I snorted softly. "And I know how to use both of them."

That only made his grin widen. "Yes, you do."

I also swapped my knife for the one the Fae man carried and followed Tavian deeper into Spring Court territory.

9

ZARED

"This place stinks of flowers," I muttered. Everywhere we went, the city smelled of them. They cascaded off balconies and spilled out of pots in front of every building. Every block seemed to contain a park where they crept across the ground, over the neat grass.

I quickly lost track of how many shades of pink bloomed all over the place. Added to that, multiple shades of yellow, purple, red, blue and the gods knew what else. There were even colours I'd never seen before.

"You don't like flowers?" Tavian plucked one as we crept past and tucked it behind his ear.

"Not this much," I said. "What would anyone do if they were allergic to flowers?"

"Live somewhere else." He shrugged. "I like it, but it is more difficult to smell alphas. On the other hand, it's also harder to smell feet."

I snorted softly. "I suppose so." That probably depended on the feet.

"We're almost to the palace. We should use Silent Maiden hand-talk for a while."

I nodded and signed that I understood. He told me once that his mother was a priestess and she taught him how to speak with his hands. I'd learned from living in the Temple and communicating with Khala and the other maidens.

I felt like crap now for pretending not to understand everything she said. When we got her back, I'd apologise for being an ass. I knew how much she hated not being able to talk and I'd teased her. It would serve me right if she hated me for that.

We'd both grown up a lot in the last few months. Especially since finding out she was part Fae. I hadn't completely come to terms with that. Or the fact I was only ever going to be human. I'd grow old and die while she stayed young.

I didn't want to think about any of that, but it was inevitable. It was almost as strange as Khala fucking her mother's former lover. As far as I knew, Cavan was in love with Alivia, but she hadn't returned the feeling.

If they were all human, the whole situation would be weird. Since Fae aged differently, Cavan didn't appear much older than Khala and me. In reality, he was a few hundred years older than both of us. All of the Fae were. I didn't know exactly how old Tave was, but he didn't act like he was older than me.

Tavian signed. "The palace is at the end of this street. If everything we've seen so far is any indication, it's going to be heavily guarded. We have to wait for the right moment."

I followed him down a side street, which led to the back of the palace.

"This would be a good place for the Court of Shadows to open a portal and attack someone," I signed. "We could use the distraction to sneak in."

Tavian looked skyward, eyes moving back and forth before he shrugged. "No such luck, evidently."

That was probably just as well, because with my luck, they'd attack us instead. I had no intention or desire to die here. Not unless it helped Khala to get free. If that was the case, I'd stand straight in front of any lightning bolts. I'd readily give my life for her to escape. There wasn't a fucking thing in this world I wouldn't give to get her away from here.

"If Ryze can't open a portal here, then neither can they," I reasoned.

"That depends on the kind of magic they have," Tavian replied. "Or to be more accurate, the kind of magic the wards are designed to keep out."

"I feel much less safe now," I signed, hoping he'd pick up on the sarcasm.

He smiled. "You're safe with me."

I followed him for a couple of minutes before the smell of flowers gave way to something much less pleasant.

"Where are we going?" I signed.

"Where else?" he replied. "The back door."

It took a moment for me to realise what he meant. I grimaced. "The sewer?"

"You can handle a little bit of shit, can't you?"

"A little bit, yes. A lot of it..." I reminded myself why we were here. Khala was more than worth swimming through shit for. I didn't have to relish the idea.

Tavian patted my shoulder. "No one ever said the life of an assassin was glamorous."

I assumed that was what he signed. As far as I

knew, the Silent Maidens didn't have a gesture for assassin. Slicing his hand across his throat seemed clear enough.

The way into the sewers was via a creek that stank worse than anything I'd ever smelled before. I copied Tavian's example and pulled out a handkerchief to tie over my mouth and nose.

"This is the poorer part of the city for a reason," he signed.

"They need more flowers here," I signed back. Lots and lots and lots of them.

Tavian chuckled and led the way along the side of the creek to a wide opening that disappeared down into the darkness.

"We can talk a bit," he said out loud. "The only people here are also people who shouldn't be here." His voice echoed slightly off the sides of the tunnel, but it was mostly absorbed by thick walls and thicker water.

Although the smell was vile, the tunnel had a kind of shelf along either side, just wide enough to walk. Every so often, ladders led up to grates which let in some air, but did nothing to diminish the stench.

"I have to give Thiron credit for how well maintained the sewer is," Tavian said.

"His cousin is an irredeemable asshole, but at least he has some of his shit under control," I said sarcastically.

Tavian chuckled. "Just picture Wornar walking here instead of us."

"I don't want to picture him at all." If I did, I'd have an image of him touching Khala in my mind. Of his cock...

I shook my head. I didn't want to think about that. Feeling it through the bond was difficult enough. Not as difficult as living it of course, but fucked up anyway.

"Me either."

Tavian led the way in deeper and deeper, before he stopped to pull out a torch from his pack. He lit it by striking a flint on the wall. It wasn't much light, but it illuminated the way and cast eerie shadows that danced around us.

"Have you been here before?" I asked, trying not to let the shadows get the better of me. *That is all they are*, I told myself. Shadows of our movement and the flickering flame.

"Here specifically, no. We need to keep a lookout for— Oh. That." He raised the torch to illuminate a side tunnel. "By my estimation, that will lead straight under the palace. Fortunately I have a very good sense of direction. Most of the time."

"Most of the time," I echoed under my breath. It was the rest of the time that worried me.

"Don't worry, I'm not going to get us lost in the sewer." He started up the side tunnel.

I had no choice but to follow his flickering light.

"Is this the kind of place most assassins go?" I asked. If a person wanted to sneak into the palace, it seemed like a logical way to do it.

"Hells no," Tavian replied. "Most assassins prefer the rooftop. Or waiting until their target goes out into the city. This is a different circumstance though. They'll be looking for me on the rooftop. And if Wornar has any sense, he won't show his face in the street until he knows we're dealt with."

"So they won't be expecting—" I stopped talking when the tunnel started to rumble. "Us."

"Maybe they do and maybe they don't. We need to hurry." Tavian started to trot carefully, torch high in his hand.

"What was that?" I asked.

The tunnel rumbled again. The ground shook under our feet. "Please don't tell me there's a giant worm, or a serpent down here."

"No, it's much worse than that," he said over his shoulder. "Every so often they have to flush the sewer."

I mouthed his words as they sank in. "And by flush you mean..."

"We need to find a ladder. Now."

The water that ran past us started to rise quickly. In a matter of moments, it was almost up to the shelf we walked on.

I glanced up the side of the wall and saw the line where the water reached in the past. It was well above both our heads. If we didn't find a ladder, we'd be swept away. That would be shitty, to say the least.

A couple of moments later, water sloshed over my feet. It was frigid. I tried hard not to think about why it was lumpy. My stomach rebelled enough as it was.

"Here!" Tavian waved me forward. "It'll be a squeeze, but I think we can manage."

Torch held in one hand, he scrambled up the ladder, all the way to the top. He moved over so he was dangling off one side.

I threw myself at the ladder and hurried up just before a sudden gush of sewage poured past.

The water rose higher and higher, washing over

my feet, my legs, my torso. I half closed my eyes and gripped with all my strength to keep from being swept away. I tried not to think about things that bumped past me as they went, before they swirled away.

What looked very much like an arm struck my leg before it twisted and disappeared. I had a feeling it was attached to an entire person.

I swallowed down my last meal before it joined the rest of the sewerage.

After what felt like a lifetime or two, the water level started to drop again. The tunnel stopped rumbling.

Everywhere from my chest down was wet and sticky. Oozing.

"This is disgusting." I grimaced.

"Yes, but I didn't get you lost," Tavian said as though that made it all right.

"I don't know, but I think lost may be better than this. Did I imagine seeing a dead body float past?"

"No, I saw it too," Tavian said. "That might have been the reason they were flushing the sewer. Destroying the evidence."

I quickly felt for the bond. It was still walled off, but Khala was alive. Thank the gods it wasn't her they disposed of. I hoped it was Wornar, but that seemed unlikely. How unfortunate. The cousin of the High Lord would probably get a more dignified disposal than to be thrown into the sewer.

"We should get out of here, in case they did that because they suspected we're here," Tavian added. He started to climb back down the ladder.

"Any chance it was a coincidence?" I followed him down.

"Possibly, but I don't believe in coincidences. They know we're coming for Khala. Chances are, they're flushing more often until they can be sure where we are."

"I thought Ryze and Wornar were friends," I said. "It seems like they hate Ryze as much as Cavan does."

"Fae are complicated," Tavian said. "For all I know, they may have held some grudge for the last two hundred years, and they've been covering for it, waiting for a chance to strike out."

He exhaled out his nose. "Or it might be the new grudge Wornar made it out to be. They may simply want to keep the lost courts from waking up. I can only guess."

I sighed and adjusted the handkerchief. I wasn't sure if Fae were complicated or just pains in the ass. With the exceptions of Khala and Tave, of course.

I occupied myself by looking at the wall and the

way the shadows danced again in the torchlight. The stone was wet now. When the light glinted off carvings, I initially thought I was seeing things.

I blinked a couple of times and shook my head.

"What the hells?"

I jerked from a doze to completely awake. Every muscle in my body was on full alert, tense. Eyes wide open, listening.

"Psst, Khala," Tavian's voice whispered from the darkness.

Was I dreaming?

I sat up, eyes scanning the shadows.

"Tave?" I whispered.

"Yes, it's me. And Zared. We've come to get you out of here."

Zared too?

I lowered the walls around the bond enough to feel for them both.

It wasn't a dream. And yet, I could hardly bring myself to believe it. What if this was some kind of trick? I tempered my hopes, just in case. Hardened my heart against a potential break.

"How did you get in here?" I felt for the others. They were close, but not as close as Zared and Tave.

"Through the sewers. We managed to...acquire some clean clothes along the way. After a quick bath in one of Thiron's fountains."

"How did you find me?" I asked.

"Through the bond. It led us to the balcony," Tavian replied. "I prefer not to go back that way. They were looking for us. We were almost caught three times."

"We had to hide in the flower bushes," Zared said. "Fucking thorns." He sat down beside me. "I'm sorry. A few thorns are nothing compared to..."

The moonlight that came in through the window illuminated his hand as he raised toward me. He let it hover near my shoulder for a moment before he lowered it again.

I understood. I wouldn't want to touch me either. I was tainted. Dirty. Even after that second bath, I felt *him* all over my skin.

"You shouldn't be here," I told them. "There are more important things—"

"There's nothing more important than you," Tavian interrupted. "You're the centre of our pack.

I'm sorry we couldn't get here sooner. We will help you through this. And we will deal with Wornar and anyone else who stands in our way." He sat on the other side of me and lightly touched my cheek with the back of his hand.

I wanted to jerk away from his touch and lean into it at the same time. My emotions were conflicted, but overpowered by one pressing need. We had to get the hells out here.

"Can we go? Please?" I whispered.

They'd come for me.

"Of course we can." Tavian dropped his hand to mine and helped me up off the bed.

"Are you...injured?" Judging by the sound of his voice he'd base how quickly or slowly Wornar died on my response.

"No." Not physically. "I can keep up."

"Of course you can," Tavian said proudly. "But if you need a rest at any time, you only have to say so. All right?"

"I'll rest when we're not here," I said. If I could ever truly rest again. I still wasn't completely sure my mind wasn't playing tricks on me. I might be asleep and dreaming about both men. If that was the case, I didn't want to wake up.

I followed them over to the door on silent feet.

Tavian gestured for us to stop. He cocked his head and listened, then eased the door open.

"Wait there," he signed. He slipped out and disappeared into the darkness.

"Khala..." Zared whispered. "I wish I could..."

I shook my head and signed it, "I'm not going to tell you I'm all right, because I'm not." There was no point in lying about that, he'd know. He knew me better than almost anyone. Even without the bond, he'd understand what I left unsaid.

"What happened wasn't your fault. It was *his* fault." And mine for being an omega. But it wasn't Zared's fault.

"I should have insisted you not go to the Autumn Court with Cavan," he signed. "I shouldn't have allowed him to take you there."

"It wasn't your decision to make," I pointed out. "I went knowing the risks."

"I didn't even try to stop you." His gestures were short and sharp, showing his aggravation.

"When have you ever been able to stop me from doing something I wanted to do?" I asked. Exactly never. I was too strong-headed and stubborn for my own good. Sometimes it was an asset, it helped me get through hard times. And sometimes it got me into those hard times.

He could argue all he wanted, it wouldn't have changed anything. The only way he could have kept me from going with Cavan was if he was an alpha.

I couldn't contain the shudder at the idea that he could have ordered me not to go. What would have happened then? Cavan could have ordered me to accompany him anyway. I may have torn myself in two, obeying them both. Would one order override the other? Did a High Lord's order hold more weight? Or maybe an order given first was the stronger of the two. I had no idea, except that it made me vulnerable in a way I'd never experienced before. One that made living in my own skin harder.

"I should have tried," he insisted.

"The corridor is clear," Tavian whispered. His sudden reappearance made me jump. "Sorry," he said quickly. "Occupational hazard."

I shrugged and tried to ignore the way my heart raced. It was just this place. I'd feel less jumpy later. All right, I was lying to myself, but whatever it took to get through this next while.

"Follow me," Tavian gestured. "Stay close."

We stepped behind him. I didn't look too closely at the guards who lay on the ground, or the shining puddles of blood on the marble floor. They probably hadn't even seen Tavian coming. I couldn't bring myself to conjure any sympathy for them. They worked for *him*. That made them complicit as far as I was concerned. Not one of them tried to help me. Not one.

It felt like three days passed before we reached the end of the corridor, we were moving so slowly and carefully. Any minute now, someone would hear my heart racing, or smell my fear. Or they'd come looking for the dead guards. Or—

I stopped at the end of the corridor, completely unable to move.

"Khala? I know it's scary, but we have to get out of here," Tavian whispered.

"I... That's not it." I moved my upper body, but my legs wouldn't follow. Panic started to settle in.

"He ordered me not to run away." My voice broke as I spoke. "I can't leave." I was as frozen to the spot as if Ryze turned me into an icicle.

"Fuck," Tavian said under his breath. He took my hand and tried to pull me forward.

I took a step, but then stopped again. "I can't." Tears slid down my cheeks. "You have to go. If he finds you here..."

"We're not leaving without you," Zared said. Before I could protest, he put an arm around me, another under my knees and scooped me up.

"Maybe you can't run, but I can." He nodded to Tavian to lead on.

I tangled my hand in the front of Zared's acquired tunic and hung on while he took several tentative steps.

At first the pressure in my mind was light, but it increased with every step. By the time we reached the corner and headed into another corridor, my head was screaming.

A whimper slipped out from between my lips.

"It's all right, I've got you," Zared whispered in my ear.

"It hurts," I replied, my voice high and strained.

Tavian stopped mid-step. "Can you manage to go a bit further?"

"I... I don't know," I stammered. "You should go. Leave me here. I..."

I didn't want to spend the rest of my life here, being raped by Wornar, but I'd never forgive myself if anything happened to either of them because of me.

Oh gods, he was going to appear at any moment and kill them both. Their blood would be all over my hands.

He might make me do to them what he made me do to Cavan. He might make me kill them, just because he could. Panic became barely coherent thought.

"Not going to happen," Zared said.

Tavian looked to be thinking. "We need to make it to the front of the palace. If we can do that, we can get you out of here."

They weren't giving up, that much was obvious.

"I can... I can hold on." I had to. It was increasingly clear I had no choice. The only way to get us all to safety would be for me to endure the incredible discomfort.

I closed my eyes, gritted my teeth and did my best to ignore the pressure. Any more and my brain might explode. If it became worse, I might welcome it.

"Good girl," Tavian said. "Stay here for a moment, I'm going to clear the corridor in front of us." He slipped away into the shadows again.

A minute or two passed before we heard a shout, followed by Tavian calling out. "Run!"

With a grunt for the extra weight he was carrying, Zared turned and ran back the way we came.

Tavian was right behind us in moments. The pressure in my head eased as we approached the room Wornar put me in, but worsened again as we ran past into another corridor.

"I guess they know we're here?" Zared said between pants.

"No, I just felt like the exercise," Tavian said sarcastically. "Yes, they know we're here and they're not happy about it. Apparently they didn't appreciate me killing a bunch of them." He didn't sound even slightly guilty. If anything, he sounded like he enjoyed it immensely.

I looked back over Zared's shoulder to see a handful of guards, swords in hand, flying around the corner. Five, no, six of them. All of them looked like they knew exactly how to use those swords.

"There they are," one of them shouted. As if they couldn't all see us bolting through the shadows. Moonlight spilled in through the windows that lined the corridor. There was nowhere to hide.

"Put me down," I insisted.

"We're not leaving you behind—" Zared started.

"No, you're not," I agreed. "Put me down."

When he finally did, I turned and gripped a bunch of magic. I focused for a moment before coating the floor between us and our pursuers with ice.

I could have incinerated them without a second thought, but I wanted to slow them down. I wasn't ready to kill that many people in cold blood. Not yet.

Not unless they gave me a reason to. They worked for Wornar, but they weren't him.

There was a chance, however slight, they didn't know what he was really like, I'd give them the benefit of the doubt. For now.

One by one, they slid and slipped. One slammed straight into the wall and let out a grunt. Several fell on their asses and growled in pain and frustration.

Tavian laughed. "That's fucking awesome. It's only going to slow them down for a minute or two."

They were already climbing to their feet. A couple of them managed, only to slip and fall again.

I froze their shoes to the floor.

They struggled to pull their shoes free, or pull their feet out of them.

Under other circumstances, it would have been hilarious. Considering what would happen to me if they caught me again, I couldn't bring myself to raise a smile.

One pulled out a knife and aimed it.

I squinted at the blade. It turned bright red and melted it in his hand before he could throw it.

The scream of agony as the hot steel poured down over his fingers was one I'd hear for the rest of my life.

Blame Wornar, I thought. *He didn't tell me I couldn't use magic against anyone else.*

"Remind me not to piss you off," Tavian said admirably. "That looks like it fucking hurts."

"Good," Zared snarled. "They all deserve it."

The sound of footsteps approaching from the other direction told me we had more company. Another handful of guards appeared around that corner. They took one look at their companions still scrambling on the ice, and drew their swords.

"Unless you want to end up like them, I suggest you get out of the way," Tavian said to them. He sounded very calm. Almost enough to silence my own panic.

"Lord Wornar is coming," one of them said. "You're not going anywhere."

I shuddered. Not just at the thought of seeing him again, but at the way my body responded to the mention of him. It was somewhere between recoiling and pure need of him.

"Lord Wornar can kiss my ass," Zared muttered.

I acted without thinking. I didn't know my hands had moved until they were in front of me. I didn't know I'd tapped into any magic until it was full of it. I could have frozen them all, or boiled them on the spot.

Instead, I opened a portal right in the middle of where the guards stood. One minute they were there and the next they were replaced by an opening.

I couldn't tell where it led and I didn't care. All I knew was that it would stay open until I closed it again. This might be the only time in my life it worked, but it worked now and that was all I gave a fuck about.

"You're going to have to push me," I said, my voice tight with concentration.

"Gladly." Tavian and Zared both grabbed hold of me and pulled me through the portal.

I slammed it closed behind us.

11

KHALA

*T*he pain was excruciating. I felt as though my skull was going to cave in on itself. My body was going to rip itself apart. Nothing existed except agony and the burning need for it to end.

If it wasn't for Tavian and Zared holding onto me, I would have opened a portal and gone back. I would have thrown myself at Wornar's feet, because that was what my instincts were begging me to do. He'd take away my pain.

But I let them hold me, because I'd rather die than give myself back to him.

"You're going to be all right," Tavian said. "You're safe here. Ryze and Cavan will be here soon."

"What the fuck are they going to do?" Zared snarled.

"A lot more than us arguing with each other will," Tavian snapped. He shook his head at Zared before turning his attention back to me. "How far away are they?"

"I don't know," I sobbed. "I can't... I can't...." All my walls around the bond were shattered, but I couldn't feel past the pain. The four of them were on the other end, that was all I knew. That and some vague sense that they were trying to reassure me.

Except for Vayne, who seemed irritated, as usual.

"Khala." Tavian put both his hands on my cheeks.

I jerked away from his touch. That had nothing to do with the strain of the alpha-order. It was pure reaction to what Wornar did to me. I barely tolerated being held down, but the intimate contact was too much.

"Fuck." Tavian dropped his hands back to my arms. "I'm sorry. Hold on a little longer."

"Where are we?" Zared asked. I'd never seen him look so helpless. I knew if he could take my pain, he would.

There was nothing he could do and we both knew it.

"Just inside the border to the Summer Court,"

Tavian said. "I could throw a stick and it would land in the Spring Court. For some reason, the portal came here."

If I could speak, I'd tell them exactly why. This was the place I would have been safe from Wornar if I'd only run a few more steps before he caught me. What he did to me wouldn't have happened. Unless he went back on his word.

I didn't bother to think how likely that was. I was here now, and safer. This might also be as far as I could go without being literally ripped apart by the order.

"So it's not—" Zared started to say.

I startled violently and squealed at a flash of light in the corner of my eye. The sight of a portal opening made me want to get up off the ground and flee.

Until Ryze stepped through, followed by Vayne and Cavan. They were all by my side before the portal even shut.

All shared the same expression. If Wornar was in front of them, he'd last another half a heartbeat before they ripped him to pieces.

"Gods, Khala," Ryze said softly. "He's going to regret the day he took his first breath."

"We need to undo this," Cavan said briskly. "Khala, listen to me. Look at me."

I turned to look at him through a haze of pain. His blue eyes were intent on mine. Whatever he planned to do, he looked confident, self assured. That reassured me in a way no words could have.

"As one of your alphas," he started, his tone firm and commanding, "you will forget everything Wornar ordered you to do, think and feel. You will put what he did to you in the back of your mind. If you think about it, remember it's in the past. He can't hurt you ever again. Furthermore, you will *never* accept an order from another alpha, including myself, for as long as you live. Our words will be nothing but words."

His order settled on me. The pain gradually evaporated, leaving only a dull ache behind my eyes.

"I should have thought of that," Ryze muttered. "Making sure she's never susceptible to any other alpha ever again."

"I wasn't sure if it would work," Cavan admitted. "I've never needed to try anything like this before. You should try giving her an order, but later. She's been through enough for now." He stroked the inside of my wrist with his thumb, but made no move to do any more than that.

"I'll give Tavian the same order too," Ryze said. "I don't want either of them to be vulnerable to some asshole like Wornar."

The mention of his name made me flinch, but the order went further than keeping me safe. When Cavan ordered me to forget what Wornar made me do, that was more or less what happened. Some of it I remembered. Some of it I didn't. The pain of that ordeal was reduced. It wasn't gone, it would never be fully gone, but it wasn't as raw.

In a way, I was glad he didn't make me completely forget. What happened was something I had to deal with and move past. Erasing it from my mind meant I didn't get to do that. My mind wouldn't remember, but my body would. I needed to heal both of them. Only time could do that.

"Thank you," I said softly. "Thank you for coming for me."

"I'm always ready to come for you," Tavian said with a small smile. "Which you may not be ready for for a while, and we all understand that. We're here to give you everything you need, including space."

"Exactly," Ryze agreed. "Anything you need, no matter what it might be, you only have to ask."

I wiped tears off my cheeks and nodded. Tavian was right, it was going to take some time before I could bring myself to be intimate with them again, but someday I would. Because I wanted to, and because if I didn't, Wornar won. I wasn't going to let him win.

"We should get the keys together and open Nallis," I said. "Figure this out once and for all."

They exchanged glances.

"We didn't get the key," Cavan said. He briefly explained how Harel switched them before we went into the throne room.

"Harel is a smug fucker," Vayne growled.

"Like most Fae," Zared muttered.

"Most, but not all," Tavian told him.

Zared looked back at him for a moment before nodding. "Yes, not all."

"I, for one, am epic," Ryze declared.

"If you say so," Vayne said to him.

"I do say so," Ryze agreed.

"Anyway," Tavian said. "We may not need the keys. There may be another way through the mountains that doesn't involve going through Nallis or the mists. At least, we could sidestep most of the mist."

When we all turned to look at him, he nodded at Zared.

"We found carvings on the walls inside the sewer," Zared said. "In the same symbols as the temple in Havenmoor. The Silent Maidens' hand language. It spoke of a tunnel in Nallis and where to find it. The symbols looked old. Worn down by the flushing of the sewer. But we could read them clearly enough."

Tavian hummed his agreement.

I stared at them. "Who would leave carvings in there? Was it always a sewer?"

"For the last thousand years it has been," Ryze said. "Whoever put it there either didn't want it seen or knew it would be some day."

"Wait a moment." Zared stared at him. "Are you saying that some Fae thousand years ago had a vision of Tavian and me going into that sewer and left carvings for us to see?"

"Is that honestly the strangest thing you've ever heard?" Ryze asked. "I don't think it's even the strangest thing I've heard *today*. Someone from the Court of Dreams knew you were coming and wanted you to find that. And you did. I suggest keeping your eyes open for anything similar that might have been left for you. For any of us."

"The Fae of the past is a fucker too," Vayne growled. "If they saw what happened to Khala and all they did was leave symbols behind..."

"They may not have known that part," Cavan

pointed out. "If they did, what could they have done?"

"They could have stopped us from going on a wild griffin chase after the keys," Ryze said.

"Exactly," Vayne said with a grunt.

"They wouldn't have known we'd jump to the conclusion that we need the keys," Cavan said.

"It doesn't matter now," I said softly. "What happened, happened. We need to focus on what happens next. Do we need to take Hycathe and Jezalyn to Nallis with us?"

"The first thing we need to do is return to the Winter Court so you can get some rest," Ryze said. "The other courts have waited this long, they can wait a little longer."

He smiled, but it was strained. He'd spent a lot of time since we met worrying about me. I'd do my best not to give him any more reason to do that.

"You're all welcome at my palace," Cavan offered. "Since we're already here, it's not far to go. And when the Spring Court notices our little distraction, we'll have a good vantage point to see it."

He smiled lopsidedly. It made him look much younger than he was. He and Ryze both had a mischievous side, although Cavan hid his better than Ryze. Ryze never tried. Never held back from being exactly who he was. It was one of the things I liked most about him.

"Distraction?" I asked. Did I really want to hear the answer to that? I'd come to realise I didn't always need to have my curiosity satisfied. Some things were better not known.

"I might have sent in a few of my most trusted men who can also use Winter Court magic," Ryze said. "Let's just say the Spring Court harbour is going to look a little icy for a while. They may have trouble getting ships in and out."

"And some of their flora may spontaneously burst into flames," Cavan added. "It's a shame to attack innocent plants, but no one takes our omega without consequences."

I smiled at the idea of both of those things happening. As distractions went, they were creative.

"That's where you were when Tavian and Zared came to get me?"

"If they got into any trouble, we would have initiated all of those things sooner," Ryze said. "As it was, we were only a few minutes away from giving the nod for them to happen." He didn't seem too disappointed it hadn't come to that.

"If you hadn't opened the portal, I would have given them a signal," Tavian told me. "It would have distracted them enough for us to run. Although, you were doing very well with your magic. You should have seen her melt a knife." He grinned at Ryze.

"That's my omega," Ryze said approvingly.

I twitched at his use of the word. I didn't want to be known for being an omega. Wasn't it enough just to be Khala?

I'd spent enough of my life being defined by what I was, not *who* I was. Silent maiden, Fae, omega. All I wanted to do was be me. That didn't seem like too much to ask.

"Can we go?" Zared asked. "Didn't you say it was dangerous out in the open?" That was a concern, but I doubted it was uppermost in his mind. His eyes were intent on me. I knew he saw my discomfort. I wasn't in pain anymore, but I was still overwhelmed with...everything.

I wanted another long soak in a bath and to take some time to think and clear my head. Not too long, because if the Court of Shadows attacked again, people may die just so I could come to terms with what happened. That didn't sit well with me. I wasn't going to mope around and let people be killed.

"Yes, let's go," Ryze stood and offered me his hand.

I forced myself not to shrink away from him. I

slipped my hand into his and let him pull me to my feet. I could tell he wanted to embrace me, but didn't know how far to push.

I gave him a quick hug and then stepped back but kept hold of his hand. The warmth of his touch was comforting.

I'd need that and more in the coming days.

12

KHALA

*A*lmost as soon as we arrived in Garial, Ryze and Cavan took Zared and Tavian aside to talk about what they found in the sewer.

I wanted to listen, but they closed ranks and Vayne escorted me to the atrium instead. He wasn't much of a talker at the best of times, but he didn't say anything until we reached the sun drenched space.

The room I stayed in when I was learning magic from Dalyth was still empty, so I slipped inside and sat on the edge of the nest, my legs hanging over the side.

Vayne followed me in and sat beside me, his movements and expression heavy.

"The others are going to say the same thing, but I blame myself too." His tone was just as heavy. "It's my job to anticipate threats. I saw the way Wornar looked at you when he first saw you. I should have seen it for what it was. I thought he was just looking at you because you're beautiful, not because he..." He shook his head.

"No one else saw it," I pointed out. I'd noticed Wornar's appreciative glances, but hadn't thought much about it either. I had my hands full enough as it was and that was before Cavan was part of my pack.

At some point, we'd have to sit down and talk about that, because that was how I thought of him, but the others may not. Except Tavian. He seemed open to anything, as long as I was happy.

"All the more reason for me to be on guard against him," Vayne groused. "We should have tried a direct approach to getting that fucking key."

"Like marching an army up to Harel's door and demanding it?" I asked, only half teasing.

"Exactly," Vayne agreed. "What's the point of having an army if you can't flex your muscles once in a while? Ryze would do anything to avoid a war, but as far as I'm concerned, Wornar declared one when he touched you." He gave me an unexpectedly tender glance.

"You're not going to invade the Spring Court over what happened to me," I told him. "How many innocent people would die as a result?"

Vayne sighed. "That's the problem with war, you can't just kill the guilty. And of course the guilty hide behind the innocent."

He crossed his booted ankles. "I promise you this — if any of us gets the chance, Wornar is a dead Fae. I'm tempted to fight the others for the privilege, but in the end it doesn't matter how the fucker dies, as long as he dies. Painfully."

I leaned back against the headboard and sat cross-legged. "Good, because you'd have to fight me too." Although, I admitted to myself I didn't know if I could deliver the killing blow, no matter how much I hated Wornar.

Vayne grunted. "I'm not going to fight you, but we know I'd win anyway. Unless you used magic, in which case I'd be fucked." He gave me a glance which bordered a smile. It was the closest I'd ever seen him come to doing that.

"I'll bear that in mind. I'll use every advantage I can get, fair or unfair." I picked at a thread on the knee of my pants.

"That must be a thing amongst people who can use magic. Ryze would cheat if given half a chance too." He grimaced.

"I don't see it as cheating," I said. "Just using what the gods gave us."

Vayne nodded slowly. "So if we have a fight, I get to use my good looks?" His eyebrows twitched.

"That really would be cheating," I told him. "Totally unfair to us ordinary looking folk."

He grunt-laughed. "There's nothing ordinary about you. You're even more beautiful than I am. I realise that's saying a lot, but it's true." One side of his mouth rose slightly.

"I don't feel very beautiful right now," I admitted. "I feel messy and... Like maybe I'll never be clean again."

He looked down at his feet, then back up again. "Can I tell you something?"

"Anything," I said. I wondered if maybe these feelings were too big for him, at least for this early in our relationship. He wasn't as open about things as Tavian, Ryze and even Zared. Or Cavan for that matter.

Vayne cleared his throat. "When I was a young Fae, maybe around fifty or sixty years old, there was a woman. She was a friend of my mother. I knew her ever since I was born."

He shook his head slowly, and his eyes glazed as he thought back.

"One time when we were alone, she decided to touch me. She was like an aunt to me and I didn't want to...but she pushed and told me it must be what I wanted because my cock...you know."

"I know," I said quickly. It wasn't difficult to understand what he was trying to say. "She made you be with her."

"Yes. I never told anybody because I think they'd just, you know, agree with her. That I must have wanted it."

"You didn't?" I asked gently. My heart ached at the expression of pain in his eyes. The memory was a difficult one, especially to deal with alone. Telling me now must have taken a lot from him. I was touched that he trusted me with something this traumatic and important.

"No." He looked back down at his feet. "Afterwards, I felt angry with myself. With her. With the whole fucking world. I've been angry ever since."

"You had every right to feel that way," I assured him. I reached over and lightly placed a hand on his leg. "What she did to you was the same as what *he* did to me. There's a difference between your cock wanting something and you wanting it. She was wrong to do what she did." Very wrong. "Is she still—"

"Alive? No. She died about a hundred years ago now. And good riddance. But I still remember how... messy I felt. Ever since then, I haven't let anyone get close to me. Not until you." He placed his hand over mine.

I offered him a smile. "Thank you for telling me. I'm sorry for what she did to you." I couldn't help asking. "Did you kill her?"

Both sides of his mouth twitched. "No. I kinda wish I had, but I didn't. She got old and sick and died in her sleep. As far as I know, poison wasn't involved. Don't quote me on that though. She had a few enemies. By the time she was gone, not too many people regretted the loss. Granted, that happens a lot to us Fae. If you live long enough, you accumulate enemies and pissed off people. Still, she was an evil bitch, even compared to some others I've known."

"It sounds like she would have gotten along well with...*him*." I couldn't bring myself to say Wornar's name.

"They would have killed each other. That sounds

just about perfect to me," Vayne said. "Which is odd, because Thiron is a genuinely decent Fae. Wornar is his sister's son, but not the only one. I never gave much thought as to why Wornar was his heir. But now—" He frowned. "Doesn't make much sense. Unless Thiron has no idea what the asshole is really like."

He stroked his thumb over the side of my hand. "Don't waste too much thought on it though. We get no say in who is High Lord of any other court. Not unless we go to war with them and win. Then we can install anyone we want, but it's a high price to pay just to do that."

"That brings us right back to innocent people dying to protect the guilty." I hated the idea of Wornar ever being High Lord of anything. "What sort of power does the High Lord have?"

"Absolute," Vayne replied reluctantly. "They have advisors, but at the end of the day their word is law. If we have a decent High Lord like Ryze, we don't have too much to worry about. He tends to listen to Tavian and me. A lot of the time, he pretends he doesn't, but he does. If we tell him something he's doing is shit, he'll rethink it. He'll take all the credit, but we don't give a crap. As long as he doesn't continue. Others, like Harel, do whatever the fuck they want and they don't care what anyone thinks."

He was silent for a few moments. "I'm pissed off at Cavan for taking you to the Autumn Court, but I admit he's not as bad as I thought he was. I thought he was like Harel. Turns out he's a lot more like Ryze. Arrogant, self-centred, but basically decent. It's gotta be eating his insides what happened to you. At least you got to stab him for it." He quirked an eyebrow.

I snorted. "I should apologise for stabbing him. Even though I had no control over it. Maybe if I'd tried harder..."

Vayne scowled. "As far as I can tell, no amount of trying harder would have countermanded what that asshole told you to do. It wouldn't matter if you were the strongest Fae in the world, that alpha bullshit would have done what it did anyway. It's like if you fell off the roof of the palace. Nothing is going to stop you from falling and landing."

"It would if I put wind under myself," I pointed out.

"You'd still land on the wind," he said. "You'd land on something. Point is, once you start to fall, there's nowhere to go but down. Once you're dead, you're dead. Can't undo that either."

I gave him a measured look.

He frowned back at me. "What?"

"The last time I was here, when I was trying to help my sisters run away from the Summer Court, I...might have brought a fish back to life. Possibly two of them."

His head jutted forward and he blinked. "Come again? I thought you just said you brought a fish back to life?"

"That is what I said," I agreed. "With magic. I accidentally killed them." I nodded towards the reflecting pool in the centre of the atrium. "Then I touched them and they were alive."

"So...they weren't really dead?"

"Oh, they were definitely dead. Somehow I combined winter and summer magic to undo that." I raised my hand in an, 'I don't know either,' gesture, then lowered it to my thigh.

"Do Ryze or Cavan know about this?" Vayne asked.

"No. I didn't trust Cavan at the time, and it didn't seem like the right time to tell Ryze. Hycathe and Jezalyn are the only ones who know. Unless it's something lots of Fae can do?"

Vayne shook his head slowly. "As far as I know, it's not something anyone can do. Not even the gods."

He chewed on his thoughts for a moment. "This might be best kept between us for now. When we get a chance, we can tell Ryze and he can decide who else should know."

He scratched his forehead. "This is knowledge that would be very dangerous in the wrong hands. Fae have gone to war for less than a skill like that. If word gets out, everyone will want you to bring back their lost relatives."

"I don't think I can bring back long lost loved ones," I said.

"They'd want you to try anyway," he said. "Knowing Ryze, he'll want us to kill him, and have you bring him back just to know how it feels."

That did sound like something Ryze would do. How many times had they mentioned how bored Fae got being alive for so long? He might think it was worth doing, even if there was a risk he'd never be brought back.

Shits and giggles knew no boundaries.

"I'll keep it between us," I assured him. For now. Sooner or later, Ryze would have to know, if only because I hated keeping secrets. We'd done enough of that already and it cost us dearly in time and frustration.

"I should let you get some rest," he told me. "I'll

be right outside the door if you need me. Me or one of the others. Fair to say, you're not going to be alone for the foreseeable future."

13

KHALA

I woke to voices outside my door. They were low. but I recognised Vayne, Ryze and Tavian. After a minute or two, Cavan said something, then Zared.

Were they all standing guard outside?

I crawled out of my nest and padded over to the door on bare feet. I pushed it open further and peered out. They all stood near the reflecting pool, illuminated by a sun that was a finger width above the horizon. Their voices were still hushed, but there was urgency in their tones. An urgency that was immediately contagious.

"What's going on?" I asked.

They turned to me, each looking guilty for having woken me.

It was Ryze who moved first, stepping to my side. "I'm sorry, we should have taken this out into the corridor."

"Like I suggested," Vayne said darkly.

"We couldn't all listen and be near Khala at the same time," Zared pointed out.

"We could have—" Tavian started.

"Does it matter now?" Cavan asked.

"It doesn't matter to me," I said. "Is someone going to tell me what's happening? Was there another attack?"

"In a manner of speaking," Ryze agreed. "Thiron is dead."

It took me a moment for his words to sink in. "The High Lord of the Spring Court? How? Did he..."

"If you want to know if he was assassinated, that's my guess," Ryze said. "Wornar has declared himself as his replacement. He's also declared that anyone that crosses his border without permission will be dealt with."

"Executed," Vayne said.

"Yes, that." Ryze gave him a short, quick nod. He glanced at the others.

"What else?" I demanded. "If it's about me, I deserve to know."

"It's not precisely about you," Cavan said. He closed his eyes and looked pained. "He's ordered that every omega in Spring Court territory be brought to the palace in Lanrial, irrespective of age and status."

My blood froze in my veins. "So he can do to them what he did to me?" I wanted to curl up and disappear under my own skin.

"We've already put out the order that any omega is welcome in the other courts," Ryze said. "And suggested that any alpha should give his omega the same order Cavan gave you, to protect them from Wornar. Or anyone else."

"We still don't know if that's going to work," Tavian pointed out.

"It's too soon," Zared argued. "She's been through enough."

"That's up to her," Tavian said.

"Are you ready to try to find out?" Cavan asked gently.

"If it helps any other omega, yes," I said straight away and without reservation. If I could save one from going through what I went through, then I'd do it.

"Khala..." Now it was Zared's turn to look pained. "You don't have to do this."

"Yes I do," I told him. "It's all right. Ryze won't ask anything I don't want to do." I turned to him. "Will you?"

"Definitely not," he said firmly. He looked me right in the eyes and said, "Put a hand on the top of your head."

My hands remained by my sides. I felt the slightest push in my mind, like Cavan's order was shoving Ryze's aside. There was absolutely no temptation to obey.

Ryze tried again. "Touch your nose."

I smiled, my hands nowhere near my nose. "I guess it worked."

"Perfect." Ryze rubbed his hands together. "Tave, I order you to ignore and disregard any order from any other alpha, as long as you live."

"*Other* alpha?" Zared looked unimpressed.

Ryze sighed. "Fine. Tave, disregard any order from me as well. As long as it's an alpha-order and not one given as a High Lord to his Master of Assassins. Those you should absolutely regard."

Tavian grinned. "I'll disregard your alpha-orders and consider the others on an order by order basis."

"I really need to find some better subordinates," Ryze said.

"Good luck with that," Vayne told him. "There are no better than me or Tavian. Right Tave?"

"Right, Vayne." Tavian patted his shoulder.

"Do you have the same problem with your subordinates?" Ryze asked Cavan.

Cavan smiled and shook his head. "I think it's a problem unique to you. You could do a lot worse though. You don't have an heir who assassinated you."

"That body," Zared said suddenly. When we all turned to look at him he gestured towards Tavian. "We saw someone dead in the sewer. They floated past when the system was flushed. Is there any chance..."

"That it was Thiron? If I was going to assassinate my High Lord, I'd dispose of him quickly too," Ryze said. "That would give me time to make up some kind of story."

"What does this mean for us trying to find the Court Of Shadows and the Court of Dreams?" I asked.

"It means he'll try to stop us," Cavan said. "Worst case, he'll ally with Harel and they'll both try to stop us."

"Is there any chance they're right?" I asked. "That

maybe we should be trying to bury them deeper or...something?"

"It's too late for that," Cavan said. "If we try that, we'll make enemies of them both. Right now, we might assume we have an ally in the Court of Dreams. At the moment that's the best we can hope for. To help them and stop the Court of Shadows from annihilating us all."

"Who would have thought we'd end up working together?" Ryze asked Cavan.

Cavan looked back at him, his mouth slightly twisted to the side. "No one is more surprised than I am."

"It's going to be harder to get to Wornar now?" Zared asked.

"For now," Cavan said. "I promise you all, as long as there's breath in my body, I will search for a way to separate his head from the rest of him. Even if I die doing it."

"You and your personal sacrifices," Ryze said. "Is that a Summer Court thing, or just you?"

"It's not just Summer Court," Vayne said. "I feel the same way."

"It's not even just a Fae thing," Zared added. "I want to rip off his balls and choke him with them."

"Me too," Tavian said. "I'd be more than happy to sneak in and do the job tonight."

"They'll be looking for you," Ryze said. "No doubt Wornar expects you to do exactly that. We have to wait until he's not on his guard anymore. If it takes a hundred years, he will be dealt with."

"We need to get to Nallis as quickly as possible," Cavan said. "While Wornar is occupied with becoming High Lord." This was the culmination of years of work for him, but he looked less than enthusiastic. He, more than the rest of us, knew what was at stake. It might not be much consolation that at least he wasn't working alone anymore.

I doubted he appreciated the years of trying to shout and being unheard. We could try to make up for it now.

"Right," Ryze agreed. "I'll return to the Winter Court and get Hycathe and Jezalyn. I have a feeling we may be needing them." He rubbed a hand over his weary face.

When was the last time any of them got any rest? I had a feeling it was a while. I'd suggest we wait another day or two, if I thought they'd agreed to it. They all had a ridiculous amount of stubbornness in common.

"We can be ready to leave in an hour." Cavan turned to me.

"If you're about to suggest I stay here, don't," I told him. "I'm coming too. I'm just as involved in this as the rest of us."

"I was going to suggest you might need some new boots," Cavan said. "I know better than to suggest you wouldn't involve yourself. If we tried to leave without you, you'd follow."

"Yes, I would," I said. "And now I know how to make a portal that stays open, following you will be a lot easier." It wasn't that simple but none of them corrected me. They didn't need to. Whatever I had to do, I wouldn't let them leave me behind.

"Also, I'd love some new boots," I said. I didn't take the time to dwell on where mine were. It didn't matter, they were only shoes. If we were heading up into the mountains, I'd need better footwear. "Some new pants and a jacket wouldn't hurt either."

"I'll have the staff organise everything we need," Cavan said. He regarded me thoughtfully, but before I could ask what he was thinking, he nodded and left the atrium.

"Vayne, you can come with me and help me organise Hycathe and Jezalyn, and our provisions," Ryze said. "Tavian and Zared, I don't think either of you need me to tell you to stay here and keep an eye on Khala."

"No, you don't," Zared agreed. "We'll keep her safe." He looked at Ryze as though accusing him of not being able to do the same.

If Ryze noticed, he gave no sign. He slipped out of the room, followed by Vayne. Of course, he couldn't portal out from here.

"Are you sure you won't stay here?" Zared asked once the three of us were alone. "We all could. What do they need us for anyway?"

"We were the ones who saw the symbols in the sewer," Tavian reminded him. "They were meant for us to see. We might both be needed to interpret them when we get to Nallis. But you might be right about Khala staying here."

He shrugged apologetically. "You'd be safer here. Vayne could stay and—"

I interrupted him. "No. I'm coming with you. And if either of you try to insist, remember what I did to that knife." I would never do that to either of them, but it didn't hurt for them to remember I could take care of myself.

"Please don't do that to my cock." Tavian crossed his hands in front of his groin. "All three of us are very attached to him."

"Don't give me a reason to," I mock growled. I gave him a meaningful look, but smiled.

"So, about you two. You seem to be getting along well." Was it too early for a conversation about that? I couldn't take the words back now anyway, but it effectively turned their attention away from me for a while. Who knew how long that might last?

I appreciated how much they cared about me, but I wasn't a fragile flower petal, broken under the heel of Wornar's boot. I was tougher than that. I had to be.

They exchanged a glance.

"I think I speak for us both, when I say there's an attraction there," Tavian said. "But neither of us is going to choose each other over you. But..." His face turned slightly pink. "If I can have both of you, and Ryze, I'd be ecstatic."

"We're a pack," I said. "All six of us have each other, including Cavan and Vayne. Within that, as long as everyone is happy, and consenting then I don't see why we can't have whoever we want."

Zared swallowed audibly. "I only want Khala and Tavian. At least...for now." He looked like he wanted to say more, but then fell silent.

His eyes on me to make sure it was all right,

Tavian leaned in to kiss me lightly on the mouth. He did the same to Zared.

"That sounds like the perfect arrangement to me."

"Me too," I said softly. All we had to do was survive potentially bringing two lost courts back to Jorius and deal with the growing animosity from the Spring and Autumn Courts.

I was starting to miss the simple life of a Silent Maiden.

14

KHALA

*H*ycathe looked at me like I was the last person in the world she wanted to see. Since that was basically her default expression, I shrugged it off. The smile I gave Jezalyn was genuine though. She was sweet. In time, the alpha woman and I might even be friends.

If Hycathe lightened up, we might be friends someday too.

"Jezalyn has ordered Hycathe not to listen to any other alphas as well," Ryze said. "All three omegas will now be able to ignore us and do whatever the hells they want."

Vayne grunted and Tavian grinned.

"Isn't it adorable that he thinks we didn't already do whatever the hells we want?" Tavian asked me.

I smiled. "Definitely. It's like he hasn't met any of us."

Ryze shook his head indulgently. "Your impertinence is so cute. I can't decide whose ass I want to smack more."

"He's such a flirt today. Is it because you now have some competition?" Tavian's gaze slipped over to Cavan.

"I'm always a flirt," Ryze said. He turned to Cavan. "Your portal or mine?"

Cavan hefted his pack higher up his shoulders. "Does it matter?"

"It might," Ryze said. "My portal might be better than your portal."

"I don't think it's possible for a portal to be better than another one." Cavan gave him a funny look.

Tavian sighed loudly. "I hate it when daddy and daddy fight."

I put a hand over my mouth to stifle a laugh.

"See, you've upset the omegas," Ryze said.

"Are we going to stand here wasting time, or are we going?" Hycathe asked. "Because we all have better things to do than listen to you argue."

"I think what she's trying to say is that someone needs to open a fucking portal," Vayne said.

"Yes, I got that," Ryze told him. "All right, I'll do

it." With a snap of his wrist, he split the air in front of him.

The tunnel on the other end of the portal was dark. Not completely dark. It was light enough to see where to put one foot in front of the other, but it wasn't the bright, icy illumination I was more used to.

"It's further to Nallis than anywhere I've taken you before," Ryze explained. He must have seen the expression on my face. "It might feel disconcerting walking through, but it should be perfectly safe."

"Should be?" Hycathe repeated. She looked disbelieving.

"It's a magic portal, there are no absolutes," Ryze told her. "Especially with missing courts opening portals in the sky. While the chance of anyone making another that dissects with mine is slim, it's not impossible."

"What happens then?" Jezalyn asked. She moved closer to Hycathe and looked as though she was about to refuse to let her come with us.

"I have no idea," Ryze said lightly. He glanced at Cavan.

"I don't know either," Cavan said. "I'm assuming it won't be good, so we should hurry." He punctuated his words by turning and stepping into the portal.

"That kind of bravery is kinda hot," Tavian said. He grabbed my hand and Zared's in his and we all stepped inside together.

Ryze was right, it was disconcerting inside. The further we got, the darker it was. The only sounds were echoing footsteps and my heart racing in my ears. Both were unbelievably loud. For the longest time, I thought we might have been the only creatures in the world. Eight Fae and one human.

Ryze closed the portal behind us. We were plunged into darkness which lasted for a minute or two before he and Cavan illuminated the tunnel with magic.

I almost wished they hadn't. The way the light bounced off the walls, never quite penetrating the shadows, made my skin crawl.

"Sometimes I wonder what it would be like to be stuck in a place like this forever," Tavian whispered. "How long would it take for me to completely lose my mind?"

"Less time than it would for the rest of us," Vayne told him. He followed a handful of steps behind. "You already have a headstart on being crazy."

"Thank you," Tavian said over his shoulder. "I love you too."

"That perfectly illustrates my point," Vayne said. "Only Tave would take that as a compliment."

"You didn't mean it as a compliment?" Tavian asked. "I wonder what it would be like to kill someone in here." He seemed to be seriously considering the suggestion, but a smile tugged at the corners of his mouth.

"If you don't shut up, you're going to know how it feels to *die* in here," Hycathe told him.

Tavian laughed. "Have you ever thought about becoming an assassin, Hycathe? You could slice open people's veins with that tongue of yours."

Whatever she thought of that, I didn't know because we were suddenly faced with daylight so bright, I had to blink for a while to let my eyes get used to the glare.

My hand still in Tavian's, I stepped out into a late morning that was considerably cooler than the Summer Court. The air was crisp and refreshing.

Cavan was already standing a few metres away, his eyes on what I assumed was Nallis.

I expected something that looked like one of the temples in Fraxius, but this was nothing like that. It was nothing like anything I'd ever seen before. My breath caught in my throat with awe.

Made entirely of dark stone that seemed to

absorb the sunlight, the base of the building was rounded. Every few metres a groove was set into the surface for rainwater run-off.

Three towers jutted out of the centre of the building. Each was shaped like the wing of a butterfly made from iron latticework, which gave the appearance of fine lace.

"It's so old, no one knows who built it," Cavan said thoughtfully. "There's nothing like it anywhere else in the world. Not on this continent, anyway."

"Some believe it was built by the gods." Ryze stepped out of the portal and closed it behind him.

"What do you believe?" I asked, addressing the question to all of them.

"I believe whoever built it was a master," Cavan said. "If they were still alive today, they'd be extremely busy creating wonders like this." He was clearly in awe of the creation.

That was understandable. I couldn't even begin to imagine how they did the ironwork, much less made towers that looked like wings. And the stone—I'd never seen stone so dark and imposing, but beautiful at the same time.

"There are ruins in a remote part of the Winter Court that use a similar stone," Ryze said. "They were built close to the coast and smashed apart by centuries of storms and massive tides. This has lasted by being isolated. Unless you count that." He pointed behind me.

I turned slowly to look.

"Oh." The side of the mountain dropped off into a thick wall of mist.

"It's closer than it was the last time I was here." Ryze looked more concerned than I'd seen him before.

"You're right," Cavan said. "It is." He gripped the handles of his pack and stepped toward the edge of the mountain.

For once, Ryze didn't claim he was always right. He frowned and watched the other High Lord like he was worried he'd disappear, never to be seen again. If he wasn't careful, I might start to think he liked Cavan after all.

They seemed to have come to some unspoken agreement between them to get along with each other. Although, they still needled each other as well. I suspected that was a habit they wouldn't break, possibly ever.

"Maybe you shouldn't go too close to the edge," I suggested.

After all the years of trying to be heard, we didn't want to lose Cavan to what was surely just a thick curtain of air and water droplets. I couldn't blame Ryze for the way he felt about the mist. It really did look like it might swallow all of us whole. What it would do with us after that, was anyone's guess.

Cavan turned his face to look back at me and smile. "It's harm—"

He gaped at something behind us. His eyes widened.

"Run!" He dropped his hands and headed toward the building.

"What—" I started after him a second before a flash of lightning lit up the sky behind me. That was followed by a sizzling sound and the smell of burning dirt and grass.

It missed me by a hair.

Fuck.

We bolted towards the building, zigzagging to avoid more bolts of lightning. A pair of them landed on either side of me, so close the fabric on the sleeve of my jacket singed.

Fucking gods.

I followed the others around the base of the building, to a wide doorway that was deep enough to hold all of us. Just barely.

I turned as Ryze threw a wall of ice between us

and the lightning. I caught a glimpse of a portal hovering maybe twenty metres above us.

Inside that, was a helmeted figure on the back of a winged creature. I'd never seen one before, but I recognised a griffin from pictures in books.

Before Ryze put up the wall completely, I flicked off a shot of fire in the direction of the griffin's rider. They ducked and the portal slammed shut.

We all slumped against each other, breathing heavily.

"Fucking hells," Vayne growled. "Fucking griffin riding asshole." Part of the sleeve of his jacket was burnt away. "That was my favourite leather jacket too."

"I'm starting to take things like that personally," Ryze said.

"There is something very fucking personal about people throwing lightning at you," Vayne growled. He glared in the direction of the sky where the portal had been. If he could have bored a hole through the sky and incinerated our attacker, he would have. Although, an arrow would have done just as well.

I had to agree with the sentiment. "Tave? Hycathe? Are you both all right?"

"No visions this time," Tavian said. "I'm fine."

I nodded at him, then turned to Hycathe. Her face was pale, eyes wide. She grasped Jezalyn's hand which rested on her shoulder. She was trembling.

"I... I felt so powerful. Like I could have blasted them both right out of existence. But I couldn't." She shook her head.

"You don't want to hurt anyone," Jezalyn said gently.

"It wasn't that." Hycathe focused all of her gaze on her lover. "I couldn't hurt...*them*. Something was stopping me."

"Like a shield around them?" Vayne asked. He gestured towards the ice wall, which was already starting to melt.

"I don't know. I just couldn't." She didn't seem to have any more explanation than that. None of us pushed her any further.

"Whatever it was, Khala didn't feel the same way," Cavan said.

"No, she almost got him," Zared said proudly. "Or her. Whatever." He put his arm around me and gave me a squeeze before realising what he was doing. "I'm sorry, I..."

"It's all right," I said quickly. "I can handle hugs. Especially when you're telling me how amazing I am." I gave him a watery smile.

"Very amazing," he said. "The most amazing woman I ever met." He kissed my cheek lightly.

"I agree, but we should get inside before they come back," Cavan said. He placed his hands on two massive handles and pushed the pair of heavy, wooden doors inwards. They groaned in protest, but slowly opened.

"We didn't need a key," Zared said.

"Not to this part," Ryze agreed. "The outer part of Nallis is accessible to almost anyone. It's the interior we need keys for. It's... Go on inside. You'll see."

Zared and Tavian's hands still gripped around mine, we stepped through the doorway and I lost my breath.

15

ZARED

I squeezed Khala's hand and stared up. And up.

What looked like towers from the outside, were hollow. At least in part. Walkways crisscrossed far above my head. I could only guess at how anyone would get up there. They'd have to be more out of their mind than Tavian.

"This is where the keys would go." Ryze led us over to another door. At least, I assumed it was a door. It had no handle, no knob. In the wall beside it, was a set of four key holes.

"If we had the keys, it would lead up to there." Ryze pointed straight up. "There's a staircase on the other side."

"Is there another door?" Khala asked. "The carvings in the sewer, what did they say?"

I glanced around. Met Tavian's eyes. "It wasn't clear. It said..." I signed the symbols.

"Shadows and dreams," Khala interpreted. "On the underneath."

"Underside," Hycathe corrected. "Like...the belly."

"Right." Khala nodded to her. "Underneath the inside. On the underside of the outside. Beneath the wings. Four palms to open. Two to guard the gate. One to open the sky."

"I like a good puzzle as much as the next man, but what the hells does that mean?" Ryze asked.

"Are you sure we don't need the keys?" I asked. If I didn't know better, I'd think they were guessing their way through all of this. And hoping none of us got killed along the way.

When that fucking lightning was thrown at us, I ran as hard as anyone, but as close to Khala as I could. I was prepared to throw myself over her to keep her safe.

If anything else bad ever happened to her again, I wouldn't be able to live with myself. I felt like all I'd done since the Summer Court's attack on the caravan was let her down.

Letting her go with Ryze, for a start. We would have managed through her heat somehow.

Everything after that... I felt like I was hanging on by a thread. I half expected her to send me away. To tell me to go back to Fraxius and live my life without her. If that was what she truly wanted, I'd go.

I knew she didn't though. She wouldn't have gone to all the trouble to find me in Havenmoor and give me back my memories if she didn't want me.

But the doubt remained. Although I cared almost as much for Tave as I did for Khala, I couldn't keep from comparing myself to him and the other Fae men.

If I could decipher this puzzle, maybe I could start to redeem myself.

I sifted through the clues in my mind. "The underside of the inside..." I moved away from them, my gaze scanning the floor.

"Shit, he's right," Ryze said. "Underneath the inside would be something under the floor. Spread out and keep looking."

I moved slowly, keeping half of my attention on the floor in front of me and the other above.

"Here." I stopped in the middle of the building,

where the floor was decorated with a chequerboard of tiles. "It's directly underneath the wings."

They all hurried over to stare.

"There are sixteen squares," Vayne pointed out. "Are we supposed to press four of them?"

"There are four of them," Cavan said softly.

"No offence, but there are sixteen." Vayne gestured toward the floor. He started to count them.

"Cavan is right," Khala said. "I mean, you're both right. There are four sets of four."

"Four palms could mean hands," Jezalyn said.

"I don't see any trees, so hands makes sense," Ryze said. He gave Jezalyn a smile.

She returned it and nodded. "So, four of us are supposed to press one of the sets of four?"

"But where within the sets of four?" Khala frowned.

"My guess would be the middle," I said. "Right where four intersect."

"That's possible, but I have a feeling if we're wrong, we're screwed," Ryze said. "Not to mention we don't know which four of us the symbols are referring to."

"Two have to be Hycathe and Tave," Khala said. "They're the most affected by the portals opening to the other courts. And the symbols were left there in the sewers for Tave to find."

"Or for Zared to find." Tavian cocked his head at me. "You could be just as important to this as anyone."

"Possibly." That was all I could say.

"We've come this far based on clues," Cavan said. "It seems unlikely they'd keep us guessing completely."

"They haven't exactly left us a big arrow pointing in the direction we need to go, complete with implicit instructions," Ryze pointed out.

"That would be too easy," Cavan said. He crouched beside the chequerboard tiles and peered at them. He tentatively reached out and touched one.

"I don't think they're dangerous. If there were, they would have dropped out from under the feet of people who have spent the last who knows how many centuries walking over the top of them."

I thought for a moment, then stepped onto the tiles. Like he said, they didn't drop out from under me. I knelt and tapped on the floor with my knuckles. Frowned. Tapped on the floor *beside* the chequerboard.

"It's hollow."

"It would be hollow if there is a secret door under there," Ryze said.

I shook my head. "No, it's not hollow under those tiles. It's hollow over here." I tapped around in a circle. "Khala, Tavian, Hycathe, come over here."

Hycathe gave me a doubtful look, but stepped over to crouch down beside the others.

"There's room here for four hands." I traced a circle on the floor. "I think it's a good idea to get off the chequerboard." I shrugged. If it dropped out from under Cavan, that was his fault.

He gave me a look, but rose and moved away from it.

"Let's all press at the same time," I instructed.

I placed my hand, palm down against the cold stone. The other three arrayed their hands beside mine. "One. Two. Three."

We all pressed downwards.

Nothing happened.

"Maybe we should try *on* the chequerboard," Ryze suggested.

"I think I should try," Vayne said. "The riddle said that two are supposed to stay behind and guard. Stands to reason one of those would be an alpha." He nodded to Jezalyn. "Hycathe isn't leaving without her. If whoever put this in place had visions of us, they'll know that."

"Why not me or Cavan?" Ryze asked.

"If anyone was going to stop us from doing this, they'd come after either of you," Vayne reasoned. "That might be the point of the attacks. I'm in the background of this. There was a much greater chance of me ending up here than either of you two. And if it doesn't work, you can try."

"All of that makes sense to me," Khala said.

"Me too," I agreed. I shuffled aside to give him more room.

Hycathe stood and moved over beside Jezalyn. She looked relieved. Sometimes it was easy to forget she got dragged along on all of this as much as the rest of us. Maybe more. I should cut her some slack.

"Let's try this again," I said. "One. Two. Three."

The floor started to rumble and shake. The section under our hands crumbled around the circumference and dropped down a centimetre or two.

Then it stopped.

I waited, my hand still in place.

"Please tell me we didn't come all this way just for that," Hycathe grumbled.

"That can't be all that happens." Cavan frowned.

Ryze matched his expression.

"On the underside of the outside," Khala said softly.

I stared at her. "Right."

"What the fuck are you talking about?" Hycathe growled.

"The riddle," Khala told her. "The underside of the outside might mean outside of the building. Whatever we did here—"

"Did something outside," I finished for her. "We should go and find out."

She stood and grabbed my hand to pull me towards the door, leaving the others to follow.

We tentatively stepped out through the double doors, keeping our eyes open for portals in the sky. So far, the sky seemed empty. The gods only knew how long that would last.

We moved slowly around the outside of the building, looking for holes, tunnels, anything that wasn't there before. There definitely wasn't an arrow pointing in the right direction. Nothing looked disturbed. The ground didn't look broken anywhere. There was no sign of the rumbling. No sign anything happened at all.

"I'm starting to think whoever did this has the same sick sense of humour as the gods," Khala said.

"Do you think they're up to something somewhere else, while we're here trying to solve a riddle that has no meaning?"

"There's a special place in the hells for them if they are," I said. I rubbed a hand over my chin. We had to be missing something. It could be staring us right in the face, or it could be hidden by centuries of dirt, dust and grass. Were we supposed to dig? I didn't think so, but I could be wrong. Only, I didn't want to be wrong. I figured out where to put our hands. I wanted to figure out the rest too.

She snorted softly. "I hope the gods make it hurt."

I gave her a half smile and leaned back to get a good look at the top of the building. "Do you think there's a way up there?"

"Not without the keys," she replied. "Unless you can fly?"

"Unless you can fly," I echoed. "One to open the sky. Can you freeze those wings? Or set them on fire?"

"I can, but so can Ryze and Cavan," she said. "If I'm supposed to do something, it has to be something they can't do. Right?" She cocked her head at me.

I wasn't sure if she wanted me to agree with her, or tell her I had a different answer. I didn't have one.

What she said made perfect sense to me. She was special, I'd known that for a very long time. Only now she was coming to realise how special. She'd always be my Khala, as far as I was concerned. No matter what the world did to us.

"Dalyth could do the things you can," I said slowly. "That might be why they killed her. It had nothing to do with Hycathe being angry with her. They wanted to stop her from doing whatever it is you need to do."

"Wind," she said softly. "I can create wind."

"Do it," Ryze said, appearing from around the other side of the building. "Cavan and I will keep an eye out for another portal. If it's going to come, it's going to come soon."

Khala nodded and half closed her eyes. She had that expression on her face that meant she was doing magic. Pure concentration. She was even more fucking gorgeous like that.

I watched the sky with half an eye, the other on the wings on the roof of Nallis. Watched as they started to shake. Dust rose into the air, followed by chunks of stone. Small at first, then increasingly larger.

I put a hand above my eyes to protect them from falling debris.

"Hurry," Ryze said urgently.

I thought he saw a portal, until I realised the mist was rising up the side of the mountain. It seemed to have ghostly fingers, reaching for us.

Reaching for Khala.

A strange, mechanical grinding filled the air, followed by a clunk. The wings moved. slowly spreading out like a flower opening its petals. The grinding sounded again, then the wings started to move. Slowly at first, but then with increasing speed.

The ground under my feet shook so hard I barely managed to stay standing.

The wings moved faster and faster until they became a blur.

Then the ground opened up right in front of me.

"Shit!" I slithered downward as the ground slanted hard, one arm windmilling, reaching for Khala with the other.

After two tries, I grabbed the corner of her jacket. A fistful of fabric in my hand, I yanked her towards me. She staggered a couple of steps until she was close enough for me to grip her arm.

She clung to me, eyes wide as the ground became steeper and steeper.

I managed to get my arms around her before the ground virtually dropped out from under our feet.

She let out a squeal and held on tighter.

We slid and rolled, dirt and rocks tumbling with us.

"Hold on!" Khala shouted.

Wind whipped around us in a frenzy, slapping my hair across my face.

Magic. Khala slowed our descent, but there was nowhere to go but down.

I tried to shield her, but we both slid painfully over jagged rocks that threatened to shred us to pieces. My jacket was the only thing keeping me from losing most of my skin.

Finally, we hit the ground with bruising force so hard it knocked the wind from my lungs. I lay there holding her while I struggled to suck back a breath.

"Khala?"

She groaned. "I'm all right."

Another groan sounded from the other side of her. "I'm all right too," Vayne said.

"Me too," Ryze agreed. "Tave? Cavan?"

"Over here," Tavian said.

Cavan grunted something right before the sliver of sky above us disappeared.

"We seem to be under Nallis," Ryze said. The darkness was broken when he illuminated the space with his magic. A lot of the time, magic freaked me out, but this once I was glad to see it. If only to break up what seemed like complete darkness.

The air smelled stale, like it was trapped for a thousand years.

"Hycathe and Jezalyn," Cavan said. "The mist took them. I tried to seize them, but... It was though hands reached out and drew them in." He shook his head, his expression haunted. There was more to that story, that was obvious, but he wasn't going to share right now.

"I told you the mist was dangerous," Ryze said. He didn't sound triumphant. Instead, he peered around, and looked deeply troubled. "I'm not sure this is any less fucked."

I helped Khala to her feet. She and Cavan used their own magic to add a further light to the space.

We stood in a vast room, clearly not natural. The walls were constructed of blocks of the same stone as the structure above our heads. It seemed to suck in light the moment it touched.

"This isn't the sky," Ryze mused.

I wasn't the only one who gave him a questioning look.

"One to open the sky," he quoted from the riddle. "Khala opened this space, but it's not the sky."

"It might be if you live underground," I reasoned.

Now they were all staring at me.

I shrugged. "The lost courts went somewhere, didn't they? Who's to say that wasn't down?"

"It's certainly possible," Cavan conceded. "It wouldn't be the strangest thing I ever saw."

"It wouldn't be the strangest thing any of us ever saw," Ryze said. "But it doesn't explain the griffins."

I glanced over to see a thoughtful look on Khala's face. "What is it?"

"I'm not sure," she admitted. "Just a thought, but I might be wrong." She walked a few steps away, raising and lowering her hand as she went. "There has to be a way out of here."

"We certainly can't go back the way we came," Vayne said. He brushed dirt off his clothes and inspected his sleeve.

"Not unless there's a way to open it back up and climb," Ryze agreed.

"I don't think we're supposed to," Khala said. "Look." She held her hand down lower, illuminating the ground.

"Are those—" I started.

"Bones," she agreed. "And that's a knife. If I had to guess, I'd say those were Fae bones."

"Does that mean we don't get out of here?" Vayne asked. "That would fucking suck. I knew I shouldn't have followed Ryze. You were always going to get me killed horribly someday."

"While I can't deny that, I didn't predict *this*,"

Ryze said. "Should we decide now who is going to eat who?"

"I call dibs on eating Khala and Zared," Tavian said.

"No one is going to be eating anyone just yet," Khala said. She turned to Ryze. "Remember the song on the map that led to the Court of Shadows? It talked about darkness and a row of skulls." She followed the bones into the shadows until she reached what looked like a pathway.

On either side, placed neatly, was a line of skulls. They stared at us, each positioned precisely the same distance from the one before, as if someone took the time to measure them.

"That's creepy as fuck," I remarked.

"That same song also said to stay away," Ryze pointed out. "Something about deadly games and knives?"

"I'd rather take the risk of a deadly game, than sit here and wait to die," Cavan said. He walked with deliberate steps down the centre of the macabre row, chin raised like he wasn't bothered at all.

Tavian said something under his breath about bravery being hot, and followed along behind, Khala on his heels.

Not wanting to be left behind, I hurried to catch up. Ryze and Vayne walked behind me.

The trail led farther and farther away from where we landed. As we went, the ceiling became lower, the walls closer. The cavernous room became a considerably narrower tunnel.

"It smells better than the sewer," Tavian observed.

"Anything would smell better than that," I said.

"He's right though," Ryze said. "Not only does this smell better than a sewer, it doesn't smell like a tunnel."

"What do you—" I started. I sniffed. I smelled dirt and slightly stale air, but something else as well.

"Trees," Khala said. "Maybe Zared was right and the courts are underground." She didn't seem convinced.

I didn't blame her. Underground trees didn't seem very plausible to me.

"Any more of that riddle?" Cavan had stopped and was now staring at another wall. It was covered with symbols. The same as the Silent Maidens' hand talk.

Khala stepped forward to look at it more closely.

She frowned adorably. "It's all... Not quite gibberish. It looks like they carved every symbol they could think of into the stone."

Ryze rubbed his chin.

"The moon, it seems, is always full,

And casts a pall upon the skulls."

"That was written on the map. Is there a moon symbol on there?"

"There's three of them," Khala said. "Full moon, crescent moon and half-moon. Should I press the half-moon?"

I glanced down at the floor. It didn't look like it was going to fall out from under us, but neither had the mountainside. At this point, I wouldn't rule out anything.

"Maybe we should hold hands or something," Tavian suggested. "If anything happens to one of us, it will happen to all of us."

"We might end up added to the row of skulls," Vayne said.

"That's going to happen anyway if we don't get out of here," I pointed out.

"I think it might be a better idea if the rest of you stand back," Ryze said. "The song mentioned treachery. Pressing that moon might do the gods knows what."

"Shouldn't you stand back too?" I ask him.

"Someone needs to stay near Khala, and I've already volunteered myself," he said. "I'm still your High Lord. When I say stay back, you'll stay back." He turned to Cavan. "I'm trusting you to keep them safe."

Cavan nodded. I thought he was going to argue that he should stay near Khala, but he moved back, putting himself between us and the wall full of symbols.

I didn't like any of this, but I stood beside Tavian and watched with my breath held. He slipped his hand into mine and moved closer until our shoulders touched.

"She'll be all right," he said softly.

I didn't know what he was basing that on, but I nodded. If this didn't do anything, we'd be fucked anyway. We'd die down here. We'd never know what happened to Hycathe and Jezalyn. Were they still alive?

The mist had looked like a living thing, reaching out with fingers and claws. Did it also have a mouth? This whole thing was so, unbelievably fucked up. Moving buildings, rows of skulls, mists that may have eaten people. More than ever, I was regretting not running away with Khala.

"Wait," I said when she raised her hand to touch the moon.

She stopped and turned around.

I pushed past Ryze, put my arms around her and kissed her. After a moment of surprise, she kissed me back, albeit more tentative than usual.

Fucking Wornar.

I forced myself to pull back before I pushed her too far, but I looked her in the eyes and smiled.

"I needed you to know I love you," I told her. "In case anything bad is about to happen."

Her expression softened. "I love you too."

I kissed her once more, quickly, then stood back again.

"That was sweet," Tavian told me.

I shrugged and tried to ignore the way my face heated. I wasn't usually given to displays of senti-ment, especially not in front of other people, but this was important. Too important not to step up and say what I needed to say. I needed her to know exactly how I felt about her. It went so far beyond caring, it had for a long, long time.

Ryze cleared his throat. "All right. Let's try this then."

"Wait," Vayne said. "How do we know Khala is the

one who is supposed to touch that moon? Or anything else, for that matter?"

"That's a good point," Ryze said thoughtfully. "It could be meant for any of us. Or none of us."

"It was me who moved the wings," Khala said. "It makes sense I'm supposed to do this too." She was more resigned than convinced. "From what we've seen so far, if it's not meant to be me, then nothing will happen."

"Assuming they haven't changed the rules on us," Cavan said.

"That is a big assumption." Ryze rubbed his chin. "I could press it and if I die..."

Before he finished talking, Khala turned and firmly pressed her fingers down on the full moon symbol.

Nothing happened.

"That was anticlimactic," Vayne said. "I guess we all get to try."

One by one, we stepped forward and pressed the symbol. Nothing discernible happened at all.

"At this point, I'd be happy for anything to happen, rather than nothing," Ryze said.

"You'd prefer this tunnel to flood and drown us all?" Vayne asked.

"It would break up the monotony," Ryze said like it was no big deal.

"It would completely end all monotony," Vayne agreed. "Personally, I'd prefer monotony for a while longer to a watery grave."

"You're starting to sound like an old man," Ryze told him.

"That's what I get for spending time with you." Vayne gave him a faint smile. "After a while, I started to become like you."

Ryze raised his middle finger at Vayne.

Khala rolled her eyes at them.

"The end of that song," she said, "it mentioned night and day." She turned back towards the wall and placed a hand on the moon and one on the symbol for the sun. She pressed down hard on them both.

"What do you know?" Vayne said dryly. "That did nothing either."

"Do you have a better idea?" Khala asked. She looked like she was just about out of patience with us.

I totally understood that. I was just about out of patience with us too. Not to mention this whole ridiculous fucking quest. Maybe we should have left the courts to get themselves out of the shit.

All right, I understood the reasons for helping them, but I couldn't shake the feeling it might come back to bite us in the ass.

"Maybe two people have to press it?" I suggested. "Tavian and I found the symbols that led us here, maybe we're supposed to do it."

Tavian grinned suggestively.

I smiled back at him. He was too fucking adorable. Being around him made my cock twitch just as much as it did around Khala.

"Let's start with this first." I moved past Khala and placed my hand on the sun.

Tavian placed his on the moon.

In unison, we pushed down on the symbols.

The response was immediate. The whole wall trembled, then started to move to one side. Something shot out of the gap and struck me in the chest.

Tavian ducked and another struck Vayne.

I glanced down. I barely had time to register anything at all before my whole body began to turn to stone.

KHALA

"*O*h my gods!" I stared in horror as Zared and Vayne both became encased in the same black stone. It happened so quickly they both barely registered their shock and horror before they were consumed entirely.

The whole thing took only several, silent seconds. Neither men let out so much as a sound. Their jaws dropped and then they were gone, obscured and still. Even the scent of fear was a flash, immediately suppressed.

"What the hells?" I threw myself at Zared, battering at the stone and trying to break it away from him.

"They're still in there. I can feel them!" Both were

confused and terrified. Their fear tangled with my own, until I wasn't sure whose emotions were whose.

Tavian did the same with Vayne. "We have to get them out of there." His tone was full of anxiety laced with guilt. If he hadn't ducked when he did...

"You cannot," a new voice said.

In my haste to try to free my men, I'd forgotten about the wall opening.

A Fae woman with hair as dark as midnight stood in the doorway, her hands clasped together in front of her. Her expression betrayed nothing but calm, the epitome of serenity.

"What did you do to them?" Ryze demanded. He and Cavan put themselves between me and Tavian, and the woman.

"I did nothing," she said. She barely even blinked in the face of accusation. "They were chosen to be guardians. They will remain as surety for your behaviour. When you have proven you will pose no threat to the Court of Shadows, they will be released. They will not be harmed."

Court of Shadows? Fuck. We were screwed.

"How can we be sure you'll do what you say you'll do?" Ryze asked.

"Because I have told you I would," she said easily.

"Because no one has ever lied before," Tavian muttered.

I put a hand on his wrist to stop him from doing anything rash. Or maybe to contain myself. Encasing two men, my men, in stone wasn't an act of welcome.

"Court of Shadows," Cavan breathed. He looked awed. "And the Court of Dreams?"

The only change in her expression was a slight dipping of her eyebrows. "We have much to discuss. Follow me." She turned in a flow of skirt and long tunic, both black with slashes of gold through the fabric.

"We can't leave them here," Tavian argued. He looked ready to pull out a knife and chip the stone away from Zared and Vayne, bit by bit if he had to.

"They will remain here and be unharmed," the woman said. She kept walking without looking back, clearly expecting to be obeyed.

"She smells like an alpha," Tavian muttered.

I hummed my agreement. She also smelled like a combination of chocolate and roses right after their peak. Not unpleasant, but not compelling either.

"What's your name?" Cavan asked. Of all of us, he was the least intimidated. If anything, he seemed validated after so many years. Only a glance back over his shoulder at Vayne and Zared showed his true concern. That was the first sign of anything other than animosity between them and him. The gesture would have been heartening under other circumstances.

"You may address me as Lyra," she said simply. "The High Lady is waiting."

The tunnel opened to another cavernous chamber. This one with other tunnels and doorways leading off in different directions.

In the centre of the chamber, a massive lake was surrounded by trees. Light shone from somewhere in the ceiling of the cavern. What looked like a huge full moon, hung in the centre.

"The magic of night and shadows," Ryze said softly.

Lyra stopped and turned to look at him. "Some call us the Court of Night. Or the Court of Darkness. We prefer shadows, because the other two suggest the absence of light. Shadows cannot exist without illumination."

"Night cannot exist without day," Cavan said.

"Indeed," she agreed. "But there is no Court of Day."

"There's no Court of the Sun either," Ryze said.

"Some would say there are four courts which live in the sun," she said indifferently. "But this is a conversation for another time. Best not keep the High Lady waiting." She clicked her tongue and turned to hurry on.

She led us around the edge of the lake, to a wide doorway that led into a grand chamber.

I stepped inside and gaped.

The walls were entirely covered with a mural that looked like a garden from the Spring Court. Amongst the flowers, trees with autumn foliage nestled. Leaning over to smell bright yellow roses, was a Fae girl with pale blonde hair the same shade as Cavan's. A man stood near her, his eyes closed as though asleep, dreaming. Shadows reached across the ground behind him.

Behind them, buildings that looked like the Winter Court palace sat amongst wispy trees, each covered in a dusting of snow.

"All six of the courts in one," a woman said. She rose from where she sat on a plush chair with high arms. Her hair was as dark as Lyra's. She was dressed in a flowing skirt and tunic in the same style. Where Lyra's eyes were blue, hers were brown.

She turned to Lyra and smiled fondly. "Thank you, my love."

Lyra returned the smile, then sank into a chair to the side of the room.

"Let me introduce myself. I'm High Lady Vernissa. We've been expecting you for quite some time." She addressed the statement to Tavian and me.

Tavian stared at her. "You're an omega."

"Of course I am," she said with a tinkly laugh. "So are you. Both of you. And your alphas are your protectors."

Ryze looked amused. "That's more or less accurate. I'm High Lord Ryzellius of the Winter Court. You can call me Ryze." He introduced the rest of us.

Vernissa looked surprised.

"I assumed things had changed in the last thousand years, but I didn't expect you'd have alphas in a superior role to omegas." Vernissa exchanged glances with Lyra.

Lyra looked downright offended.

"This is what I've been trying to tell Ryze for the last two hundred years," Tavian said.

"I'd laugh, but he really has," Ryze said dryly.

"Likely it was something akin to suggesting he'd make a better High Lord than you, not that omegas should be in command," Cavan said. He looked like he couldn't decide what to make of all of this.

"So, you mostly have women leading?" I asked Vernissa, trying to make the question sound innocuous. That was an idea I could appreciate. I didn't see a reason for any particular preference toward men leading.

"I've been High Lady for five hundred years," Vernissa said. "Before me, it was my aunt. She was the one who found this place, to keep us safe from the Court of Dreams."

"Court of Nightmares," Lyra said sourly.

"Legend has it that *you* were trying to destroy *them*," Ryze said, the slightest hint of accusation in his tone.

"Legend *they* started," Lyra said, just this side of snippy. She sniffed, then pushed her mask of serenity back into place.

"The Court of Dreams captured and trained griffins for the sole purpose of invading and destroying us," Vernissa said. She seemed more accepting of the past. She'd certainly had time to get used to the idea. "They forced us into hiding, before the seasonal courts did the same to them. They've been trying to find us ever since."

"Why did they try to destroy you?" I asked.

If they were to be believed, everything we were

told was backwards. Unless they were full of shit. They seemed sincere. Although, that's how I'd act if I was trying to get sympathy. I'd keep my judgment to myself for now.

"That's a long tale," Vernissa said. "I've been remiss as a host. Let us share a meal and I'll go into further detail."

"Actually, what we would like is for you to remove Zared and Vayne from the stone," I said. "They are our pack. We need them with us." I glanced at Tavian, who nodded.

"Right. They're along to protect us." He forced a smile, but looked like he might start stabbing if they didn't agree to our request.

"I apologise," Vernissa said smoothly. "I cannot undo that magic until we come to an understanding. I can assure you, they are well and alive. But you know that, because your bond with them is intact." She addressed that to me.

"They're alive," I agreed. "But they're terrified." I did my best to assure them, but it did little to calm their minds. If they could smash their way out, they would. Hells, if anyone could glare their way out, it would be them. Doubtless they'd tried.

"Then we better talk quickly." Vernissa gestured

for us to follow her through a side door that led into a narrow room with a long table in the middle.

Fae, all with dark hair and clothes, bustled about setting down plates and pottery cups. A large teapot sat in the centre of the table, beside a tiered tray full of cakes.

For the first time since we stepped out of the tunnel, I saw Fae men. Their hair was as dark as the women, and just as long. The same dark skirts brushed the tops of their feet.

They moved around with their eyes down, each step silent as though trying to be as unobtrusive as possible. This was a stark contrast from any man I met in the seasonal courts. Or in Fraxius for that matter. None of the priests in the Temple at Ebonfalls were subservient like this.

We sat, they served us cake and tea before they hurried out.

"People who work for you and don't talk back," Ryze remarked with a side glance at Tavian.

Vernissa laughed her tinkly laugh. "They don't work for me. I own them."

We all stared at her then.

"You...own them?" Cavan asked. He glanced at me, but then away again before I could dig my elbows into his ribs for whatever he seemed to be thinking.

Fae men.

"Of course," she said lightly. "Some of them used to belong to my aunt. Some of them are sons of those men."

"Are all the men in this court owned?" I asked carefully.

"Oh no, not at all," she said with a wave of her hand. "Merely those born to it, or who choose to surrender themselves. It's not easy to live underground the way we do. Many have long struggled with my aunt's decision to confine the court to these caverns. They want to see the sunshine and feel the wind on their faces. And they will soon enough. But there is much to be considered first."

"If you didn't send the griffins, were you the ones who put the symbols in the sewer of the Spring Court?" Tavian asked.

She gave him a blank look. "We've had minimal interaction with the seasonal courts for the last thousand years. The first warning we had of your arrival was when the cavern above us moved."

"The Court of Dreams did all that?" Tavian surmised. "Because they wanted us to find you."

"They wanted someone to find us," Lyra said. "Be

it you or them. Undoubtedly, they're tracking your progress."

"They tried to attack us aside Nallis," I said. "They didn't seem to want us to find you at all."

"The fact they didn't kill you suggests they were merely trying to scare you," Vernissa said. "That is the manner in which they behave. With aggression and force."

"You don't seem worried they followed us here," Cavan pointed out.

"No one can enter here without our knowledge," Vernissa replied. "If they tried, they could only enter several at a time. We'd deal with them before they became a problem."

"By turning them to stone?" I asked bitterly.

"That's certainly a possibility," she agreed. "The presence of your betas will provide additional warning. Hence they are the two guardians. The magic that holds them in place will respond to any further incursion."

"You said you want to come to some kind of understanding," Ryze said. "Let's cut straight to that. I don't want my people in stone any longer than necessary."

I murmured my agreement. As far as I was

concerned, them being in stone in the first place was longer than necessary.

"Yes," Cavan said. "What is it you want?"

"We want to return above," Vernissa said. "We've spent enough time underground. It's time for us to regain our place in the sun."

"What do you make of all of this?" Ryze asked us. We'd finished our tea and cake with small talk before Vernissa insisted we rest. Further discussion and negotiation would take place after that. Both High Lords tried to steer her back to her declaration, but she wouldn't be drawn.

Cavan was pacing back and forth across the room, arms crossed, frown on his face.

"I spent a lot of time thinking about all of this but nothing is the way I visualised it. Everything I ever knew painted the Court of Shadows as the antagonist. Including those songs on Ryze's maps. Now they're suggesting all of that was incorrect?"

Ryze reclined on the wide nest in the middle of

the room, hands behind his head, legs crossed at his knees. Even piled high with cushions, it was big enough to sleep ten people comfortably.

"In my experience when dealing with two opposing points of view, the truth is usually somewhere approximately in the middle." He glanced meaningfully in Cavan's direction.

"Is that your way of admitting you were wrong about Cavan?" Tavian asked. He'd guided me over to a couch that sat against the wall and pulled my feet onto his lap. He took off my boots and started to massage my feet.

"To some extent," Ryze said. "As wrong as he was about me."

Cavan stopped pacing to quirk an eyebrow at Ryze. "I'm not entirely certain I was wrong. But you are more tolerable than I expected."

"That's not surprising, I'm extremely tolerable." Ryze uncrossed his legs and crossed them the other way.

"Yes, you are," Tavian told him.

Cavan snorted softly.

"It looks like we have a way to go." Ryze shrugged.

"At least they're trying," Tavian said to me.

"We should be trying to get Vayne and Zared out of the stone," I said. Neither was as frantic as they were before. In fact, they seemed to be asleep, or perhaps unconscious.

"Unless you want to try melting it, there's no way out of there until Vernissa frees them." Cavan sighed. "I hate it also, but we have no choice but to do what she says."

"Do you hate it?" I asked. "You seemed only too happy to get rid of Zared once before. Have you forgotten how you had Dalyth took his memories?"

He stopped pacing. His body stiffened. "I haven't forgotten. You know I only did that for his own good."

"So you said." I tried but failed to keep the bitterness out of my voice. Zared knew going to the Summer Court might end in his death, or worse, and he'd gone with me anyway. In spite of Cavan's reasoning, the whole thing still stung.

"Khala—" Cavan started.

"We've all been through a lot," Tavian said quickly. "I think we all need to relax and unwind." He massaged my toes one by one.

I exhaled softly. He was right. This was not the time to tear each other apart.

I lost myself in thought for a while.

Finally, I said, "I admire Vernissa. She seems like the kind of woman who would never let anyone take power away from her." I pressed my lips together, but they all knew what I was referring to.

"You didn't *let* anyone take power from you," Tavian said softly. "He took it. He took complete advantage of the fact you're an omega. The only person who did anything wrong was that prick. I look forward to stabbing him in the eyeball."

I managed a faint smile. I was looking forward to the same thing.

"My point is that I don't have to let him take anything from me," I said. "Including being...intimate. I don't know what I'm ready for, but if you can be patient with me, I'd like to try."

Maybe it was too soon, but I wanted to take the power back for myself. I needed the closeness with the pack I had here with me. If it wasn't for Cavan's order that dimmed the memories of what Wornar did to me, I wouldn't have been ready for anything.

Because of that, I was done being a victim. I wanted to touch and be touched. To show these men how I felt about them.

Ryze sat up. "We can be as patient as you need. Why don't we start with a snuggle?" He held out his hand.

"A snuggle sounds good," I agreed. I swung my legs off Tavian's lap and stood.

I grabbed his hand, and Cavan's, and tugged them both towards the nest. We all climbed in and lay down, Ryze and Tavian on one side of me, Cavan on the other.

For the longest time, no one moved.

I lay still, Cavan's hand on my hip, Ryze's just above.

Tavian was the one who made the first move, sliding down and undoing the front of Ryze's pants.

Ryze twisted to lie on his back while Tavian freed his erection and started to slide his hand up and down his length. He groaned softly.

"I don't expect you to call me sir," Cavan started.

"Maybe I want to." I offered him a smile. Being dominated by someone I felt deeply for was entirely different to what Wornar did to me. Consent was everything.

Cavan lifted his eyebrows. "You want me to spank you?"

His words elicited a rush of heat through my entire body. Heat that was tinged with trepidation, but made my pussy wet as fuck.

"Same safe word?" I asked.

He nodded. "Yellow it is." Eyes on mine at every moment, he unbuttoned the front of my pants and slid them with almost painful slowness down my hips. He paused every time I even looked like I was uncomfortable. A couple of times I had to smile and nod for him to keep going. Every moment, I was in control. If I said to stop, he'd stop immediately.

A couple of times I thought about it. My mind flashed me back to the Spring Court, back to another man's hands on my body. His cock...

I pushed them away. What mattered was here and now, and proving to myself I wasn't broken. Later, I may regret pushing myself too hard, but I'd worry about that when later arrived, if it did.

By now, Tavian was licking and teasing the tip of Ryze's cock. Ryze's eyes were half closed in enjoyment. It was the first time I saw them together and it was hotter than hells. Knowing they fucked and seeing it were two different things.

I kept my eyes on them while Cavan flipped me over onto my belly.

They watched me as he kissed my ass, nibbled on it then brought his hand down on my skin.

The first spank was tentative, almost gentle.

"If that's your idea of spanking..." Ryze teased.

"I'm more than happy to show you how hard I spank," Cavan told him.

"That's some wish fulfillment right there," Tavian muttered.

I hummed my agreement, but looked at Cavan over my shoulder. "How about you show me instead."

"With pleasure." Cavan brought his hand down harder the second time. And harder again the third.

I groaned from sheer bliss brought about by a combination of the stinging slaps and the sight of Tavian with Ryze's cock deep down his throat. Every slap and suck drove the bad memories further and further to the back of my mind. Nothing else existed but this.

Cavan's order was stronger than I thought; it went deeper. It kept the worst of the darkness from reaching me. More than that, it knitted that part of me back together, like magic closing a wound.

With every spank, I healed a little more.

Between spanks, Cavan slid his hand between my legs, grazed his fingers over my pussy.

The moment he touched me, I froze.

"I'm so sorry—" He pulled his hand back immediately.

"No," I said quickly. "It's all right. Please don't stop." I needed to know I could be touched by someone who respected me and my boundaries. The fact he was paying close attention spoke more volumes than the library in the Winter Court. The last thing he wanted to do was hurt me.

"When you touch me...I feel more myself again. Please..."

He hesitated for a moment longer, then slipped his hand back to trace slow, deliberate circles around, and over my clit.

I shivered under his touch. The more he gave me, the more I wanted. The more I needed.

He parted my legs a little wider and swirled his fingers several times more around my aching clit, before sliding one inside me.

"Mmmm. More of that please, sir."

"Whatever my omega wants," he rumbled. He slid in another finger, then another.

Ryze slowly bucked his hips, driving himself deeper into Tavian's mouth.

Cavan slid his fingers out of me and turned me over onto my back. He bent my knees and lowered his face between my legs. He slipped his fingers back inside me but traced swirls around my clit with his tongue.

It only took me a matter of moments to almost came apart.

"That's it," Cavan said between licks and nibbles.

"Come for me." He sucked my clit into his mouth and bit down lightly.

My whole body quivered. When I came it wasn't with a rush of intensity. Rather, it was a gentle, perfectly blissful wave of pleasure washing over my body and sweeping my soul clean.

In that moment, I knew Wornar could never hurt me again.

It wasn't until Cavan lifted his face from me that I realised Tavian moved away from Ryze and was busy undoing Cavan's pants and drawing out his cock.

My eyebrows rose. I watched, curious to see Cavan's reaction to Tavian's touch.

He looked bemused at first, but he didn't pull away. If anything, he was completely still until Tavian lowered his mouth onto his tip and started to suck.

Holy gods, that was as hot as seeing Tavian suck Zared or Ryze's cocks.

Ryze took the opportunity to roll over to me and smile before he straddled me. "I apologise for the lack of hot wax. I can get a candle if you like."

He started to stand.

I quickly grabbed his arm and pulled him back.

"Next time. Right now I just want your cock." I

manoeuvred him so he was straddling me and wrapped my legs around his hips. If spanking and finger fucking could heal me, I wanted to see what being fucked would do. I ached for it.

"Whatever the lady wants." He slowly, slowly pressed himself inside me, filling me bit by bit until he was fully seated inside. He closed his eyes and savoured the sensation before he started to slowly thrust into my body.

Like Cavan had, Ryze watched me carefully for my reaction.

All he would have seen was my enjoyment. My overwhelming need to live in this moment.

Gradually, he thrust harder, his knot sliding against my clit and driving me towards the edge again.

With a rush, I came again, this time the intense inferno that had me bucking my hips and grinding myself against him for every precious drop.

My breathy cries pushed Ryze and Cavan both over the edge, thrusting and coming inside me and Tavian.

I glanced over to see Cavan looked surprised at himself for spilling his pearly cum into Tavian's mouth.

Ryze panted, then slid out of me and rolled away, leaving space for Tavian to replace him.

Tavian lay beside me and pulled me over so I straddled him. I slowly lowered myself onto his cock. He groaned in pleasure as I rode the other omega to his orgasm, and a third for me.

I sagged down, sweating and panting, but satisfied and feeling whole for the first time in a long while.

I was right, this was exactly what I needed.

19

KHALA

*W*hen I woke, the cavern was dark and silent. Presumably they turned off the illumination to simulate night-time. According to my body clock, it was close to morning.

I felt through the bond for Vayne and Zared. They were both still alive and surprisingly calm. Even Vayne didn't seem as aggravated as usual. Maybe he was getting some much-needed rest in there.

I managed to slip out of bed without waking any of the men, and padded over to the door.

Without knowing why, I slipped out into the corridor. I headed towards the lake just as the fake moon started to glow, faintly at first. Its reflection glinted off the still water, making the whole place strangely beautiful.

I stood watching the light gradually grow brighter. After several minutes, I sensed that I was also being watched. Nothing malevolent. At least, I didn't think so.

I turned to see a Fae man, his curious gaze on me. He was one of those who served us tea and cake yesterday.

"Morning," I greeted. I spoke low to keep my voice from echoing around the space.

He nodded in response.

"It's pretty here," I said for something to say.

He nodded again.

"Are you not allowed to talk?" I asked. None of them said a word the day before. "Can you talk?"

When he didn't respond, I asked the same question with my hands.

That pleasantly surprised him, judging by the widening of his eyes.

He signed back. "I am not permitted to speak out loud to an omega. I am...beneath them. In my role here."

His gestures were different to the ones I knew, but I understood the general meaning. He was subservient to Vernissa. And perceived himself to be subservient to me and Tavian too.

"Are you allowed to speak to alphas?" I asked out loud. He could clearly hear.

"That depends on their rank. Some, yes. Some, no."

I took that to mean he couldn't speak to Lyra.

"You're a beta? What's your name?"

"Yes," he signed. "Rijal. And you are Khala." He glanced around nervously like he shouldn't be standing here too long communicating with me.

"Yes I am. Am I allowed to give you permission to talk out loud to me?" I didn't see myself as superior to him in any way, regardless of my designation.

He shook his head vigourously. He even backed up a step or two, like he was scared I'd insist.

I put my hands up to placate him. "All right, I won't ask. Why are you not allowed to talk to people of rank? Is it considered offensive?" The way some people talked certainly was.

I pushed any thoughts of Wornar out of my mind.

"It's considered rude," Rijal signed. "We're expected to know our place. To be silent. Those who rule want to forget we're here except to receive the food we bring and to see that we cleaned for them."

Again his gestures were different but under-standable.

"It sounds like they don't see you as people," I told him.

He looked down at the ground. "We are less. Those who cannot own ourselves. We are less."

"You're only less because they want you to think you are," I said firmly. "Why does she own you?"

"Because her family owned my father, and my father's father. And his father." He shrugged.

"Is there any way to stop that?" I asked. Of course, that was assuming he wanted to. He didn't seem too concerned with his circumstances. Or maybe he was resigned to them.

"If we ask," he signed.

I blinked. "All you have to do is ask?" He nodded again. "So you don't mind?"

He cocked his head slightly. "Sometimes I mind. We get punished if we're too loud. But here—" He gestured around the cavern. "There are a few ways to...live. To get food. Some hunt through the tunnels. Some go above to hunt there, or try to catch fish. Some train in the army. Some serve."

"So there aren't too many jobs down here," I concluded. "Vernissa makes sure you eat?"

No wonder they were ready to return to the

surface of Jorius. If being owned was better than starving, then what choice would they have?

"If you go back up to the surface, the whole court, what would you do?"

"I would grow food," he signed. "I would look at the sun and watch food grow."

"You'd be a farmer," I said. "That sounds fabulous." Assuming there was farmland available for him. Where would the Court of Shadows go? I wasn't even sure where it was before. I'd have to ask Cavan.

Rijal grinned. "What is the sign for this word?"

"Farmer?" I asked. I showed him the sign I knew and he copied it back to me.

"How do you know these signs?" he asked.

I could have asked him the same thing. "I guess your ancestors taught mine. Then they made sure we couldn't forget them."

The Silent Maidens seemed to be a bridge between this court and the world above. Was that intentional? Cavan once said the Silent Maidens were established as a means to eventually return the two courts to Jorius.

Someone was definitely playing the long game. Vernissa's aunt, perhaps.

"How many people are there like you?" I asked. "Are they all men?"

"There are a few thousand throughout the caverns," he replied. "All men, yes. Women are for leading, or having children. Not for serving. Is it the same?" He pointed upward.

I snorted softly. "No, it's usually the men who lead. Women serve and have children. Although some join the army or become guards. Some are even farmers."

He gaped at me in disbelief. "In the Court of Shadows, women do not grow food. Or hunt. They would get... Ground and blood on their hands."

"Dirt?" I suggested. I pointed to the base of a nearby tree, then showed him my hand symbol for dirt. "Women aren't allowed to get dirty?"

He shook his head vigourously. "No, no dirt. No mess. Only men have a mess on them."

"Only men get messy?" I said. "Some people would say men get messy more often up there. But women get messy too."

He looked horrified. "Why? Why would a woman get mess on her?"

"Because she wants to." That was the only explanation I could give. It sounded like we had more freedom than they did down here, but maybe I shouldn't judge too harshly. They did what they had to do to survive. If the lake was their main source of water, then it would be easier to stay clean than it would to wash off a mess. After a thousand years, that might have become a rule, as well as a necessity.

"Those men with you," Rijal signed tentatively. "Do you—" He made the symbol for fucking.

My face heated slightly at the direct question. "With them? Yes."

"Because you choose to?" he asked. "Because they choose to?"

I smiled. "Because we very much choose to, yes. Do you not get to choose?"

He glanced down at the ground again. "Vernissa decides who is best for breeding with whom. For the strongest. If we are weak, we don't get to fuck."

It was my turn to look horrified. "She decides who you sleep with?"

I supposed that made a twisted kind of sense too. With limited space in the cavern, those here needed to be strong enough to survive. And to fight whatever may come on their way back to the surface.

He looked confused. "Not sleep, no."

I laughed. "I'm sorry, it's another way of saying fucking. It doesn't make much sense I guess.

Although, often sleep happens after fucking. And some snuggling."

He gave me a funny look like maybe intimacy was something he wasn't familiar with.

Each court had their peculiarities, but this, this one was different again. The seasonal courts had more in common with the way humans lived than they had with the Court of Shadows. A thousand years apart had made a great deal of change between them.

I wasn't sure what they'd all make of each other. I didn't want to think about Wornar, but I couldn't shake the feeling he'd love telling his people who they could and could not screw. He'd probably find that hilarious. Asshole.

The light was brighter now and Fae were starting to emerge from various tunnels and doors.

"How many live here?" I asked.

"I think, maybe twenty thousand," he said. "So many no one is allowed to breed right now. If we do, there will be too many. Too many to feed and not enough food."

He paused for a moment before he continued. "Vernissa has announced the culling will happen in two days."

"The...culling?" That didn't sound good.

"Yes, when Fae get old and aren't strong anymore, they're culled. There hasn't been a culling in a hundred years. But for going above, she wants us at our strongest."

I closed my eyes for a moment, trying to get my head around what he was telling me.

"They kill Fae because they got too old?"

"Old and not strong," he agreed.

"What about their wisdom?" I asked. "I hope to be wise when I've been around for a few hundred years."

"I don't get to decide," he said evasively. This culling seemed to be something he approved of. Or at least was accustomed to, so he didn't question it anymore.

"How old are you?" I asked.

"Only one hundred and twenty-three," he signed.

"Young then," I said. A hundred years older than me, but not old enough to worry about the culling for a very, very long time. It was easy not to worry about something that wouldn't affect you for centuries.

"Barely more than a child," he agreed. "I was one of the last bred here. Only Leopol and Geris are younger."

My eyebrows rose involuntarily. "Does that mean

no one has fucked anyone they might get pregnant for over a hundred years?" No wonder he wasn't familiar with intimacy.

"Yes. Hands, mouth and ass only."

"What happens if someone puts their cock into a pussy?" I asked.

"They are culled," he said simply.

"How would anyone know?" Did they have any idea what we got up to last night? For all I knew, they'd watched our every move through a hole in the wall.

"The court is small, with many Fae," Rijal explained. "It's difficult to be alone anywhere. The risk... Most won't take it."

"Fucking isn't worth dying for," I reasoned. Most of my men would agree to disagree on that point. So would I, when I thought about it.

"I should go and serve," Rijal said. "If I'm late, I'll be punished." He gave me a bow and hurried away.

I watched him disappear down a side tunnel then made my way back to my room.

20

KHALA

"You want what?" Ryze stared at Vernissa. "You realise it's not in my power to give. Humans live in Fraxius, Freid and Gerian. Even if I wanted to forcibly remove them, which I don't—"

"There is no choice to be made here," Vernissa said evenly. "We cannot remain under the ground indefinitely. Unless you have sufficient land in the Winter Court, and are ready to concede power to me..."

"Not a chance," Ryze said immediately. "Land we have. Me stepping aside as High Lord is not an option. Nor is it an option for Cavan to step aside." He glanced at Cavan.

"Not a matter for consideration," Cavan agreed.

"Nor can we offer the Spring or Autumn Courts." In spite of the animosity toward both High Lords, that would likely result in bloodshed.

"The Autumn Court has an heir," I pointed out. "Illaria doesn't agree with Harel. If something happened to him, a reasonable replacement exists." I couldn't say the same about the Spring Court.

"Then the human lands remain," Vernissa said reasonably. "Are you trying to suggest Fae aren't a higher priority than humans? That we should remain down here in the darkness and continue to stagnate? We cannot continue to live like this. We are safer here, certainly, but this is a miserable existence in comparison to our former glory."

She leaned forward and tapped the tip of her finger on the table in front of her. "We held those lands. They're rightfully ours. We ruled over the humans and lived in a harmonious relationship with them."

"I thought the Fae moved out of Fraxius," I said.

"We did." She turned her eyes to me. "We moved here. None of the seasonal courts ever held land there. Only the Court of Shadows and the Court of Dreams. And now your High Lords—" she used the title like it was an insult "—are suggesting we can't return."

Ryze sat back and laced his fingers behind his head. "I'm not suggesting anything. I'm saying it outright. That land is not mine to give. It's not Cavan's. If it belongs to anyone here, it's Khala and Zared. Perhaps you could remove him from the stone so he could give his say. He might even agree with you." No one in the room believed that for a moment.

"He's a beta," Vernissa said coolly. "He will remain where he is, for now."

She turned her gaze to me. "You're an omega. And a Fae. Why is Ryzellius suggesting you have any say over our former lands?"

"I was born there," I said simply. "I—" I glanced at my three men before turning my attention back to her. "I'm part human. I transformed during my first heat."

She looked slightly disgusted, but thoughtful. "Then you know the way humans live compared to the way Fae live. Do you truthfully believe humans live better? Or do you think they would benefit from things the Fae have, like running water? We would provide them with those things."

"That's not my decision to make," I said. "Every human I know would love running hot water, but what would they be giving up in return? You said the

Court of Dreams wants to destroy you. Would you put innocent humans in the middle of that?"

"I believe we can adequately protect them if they choose to accept our protection," she said smoothly.

"Yet, you had to come here because you can't protect yourselves," Ryze said.

"With the assistance of the seasonal courts, we can adequately protect ourselves and them," she said. "It's in the best interest of all of us to work towards eradicating the Court of Dreams entirely."

"How would it help us?" Ryze asked.

"They keep trying to attack us from the back of a griffin," Tavian pointed out. "Or multiple griffins. Didn't you say that was starting to feel personal?"

"Not enough to go to war for," Cavan said. He pressed his thumb against his lips. "There's a lot to consider here. And a few pieces of the puzzle that need to be placed. The whereabouts of the Court of Dreams, for one thing."

"That's a good question," Tavian said.

"I was wondering the same thing myself." Ryze cocked his head at Vernissa. "Perhaps you can enlighten us."

"We're not entirely sure," She admitted. "We believe they may be higher up the mountain, but the summit is out of reach on foot. And protected by wards, so no one can try to portal in or out. We've sent people to climb there and look, but they've never returned. Whether that is from the court, or natural hazards, is unknown. I'm unwilling to send anyone who is bonded, because of the potential impact on their mate who remains behind."

She didn't seem too worried about the impact on me of having two of my mates encased in stone.

Lyra, who was silent until now, spoke. "I have suggested placing a bond on a pair and sending one of them. If it isn't a natural, gods given bond, it may not have the same impact."

"I haven't dismissed the suggestion, merely the idea of sending someone else after so many failed attempts," Vernissa said heavily. "It's possible the court is hiding in the mists, or somewhere across the ocean. I don't want to send anyone else on a fool's errand."

"What you mean *placing a bond?*" I asked, crinkling my brow. "You can do it without having to wait for one to form?"

Cavan was sitting forward, listening with interest.

"One of the idiosyncrasies of our magic," Lyra said. "It's not a common ability, but it's one I can perform."

"Can you do it for us?" Cavan asked, nodding towards me. "If Khala wanted to?"

"I do want to," I agreed. All this time, it was strange to be bonded to the others and not him. But there was more than just me to consider here.

"If the others agree." They had to be all right with it or I wouldn't go ahead. I wouldn't risk what I had with any of them for anything, not even a bond with Cavan.

"Definitely," Tavian said without hesitation or reservation.

Ryze eyed Cavan speculatively. "I suppose it wouldn't hurt for you to keep a connection with her when she spends most of her time in the Winter Court with me."

"That's one hells of an assumption," Cavan said. One he seemed to find amusing rather than offensive.

"I can also dissolve bonds," Lyra said helpfully. Her serene expression didn't change except a twinkling of her eyes.

"Hmmm," I hummed as though actually considering it.

Ryze frowned at me.

Tavian looked amused, clearly knowing I wouldn't break the bond with him.

"I don't want to break any bonds," I said finally.

I had a good idea what Zared would think, but I took a moment more to consider Vayne's reaction. In the end, all they wanted was for me to be happy.

"I would like to have one with Cavan."

He looked pleased. "Can you do it now?" he asked.

"You're very impetuous for a Fae," Vernissa told him.

"I wasted enough time trying to convince them you exist," he said evenly. "I think it best not to delay things anymore. If that makes me impetuous, then so be it. I don't want to wait two hundred years to have a bond with her."

"I feel the same way," I agreed. Besides, the gods only knew when we'd get another opportunity to do this, if ever.

Vernissa seemed annoyed that the conversation was sidetracked from taking land from humans, but she nodded anyway.

"It's time for a break. Do what you feel you need to do and then we'll finish this conversation. With your cooperation, we can have your other two bonded out from their incarceration before another night falls."

She rose and swept from the room.

Ryze sighed and closed his eyes. "She's under the impression all of this will be easy, isn't she?"

"It is easy," Lyra told him. "I need only to touch both of them and—"

His eyes popped open. "I didn't mean the bond. I meant the whole thing about human land."

"I know," she said lightly. "That is easy too. We must put Fae before humans. That seems straightforward to me. Are we not superior in every way? We live longer, we have magic. We don't have round ears." She wrinkled her nose.

"I like round ears," I said quietly. "Can we do the bonding? Please." I didn't want to have any more conversations like this. The whole dislike of one race for the other was frustrating. More often than not, I felt like I was caught in the middle. I looked Fae, but I felt human. More and more I started to feel like a Fae, but I couldn't forget where I came from and who my father was.

Ironic, given I could barely remember my father at all. I knew enough not to turn my back on my roots.

"Very well." Lyra rose and moved to stand between Cavan and I. She placed a hand on each of ours and closed her eyes.

"Do we have to do anything?" I asked. We were

putting a lot of trust in her. Considering she was also not bothered about having two of my lovers encased in stone, perhaps we shouldn't trust her to do anything magical to us.

On the other hand, if she tried to screw us over, she'd lose any trust Ryze might have put in her or Vernissa. Any chance of being allies would be shattered.

This might be their way of trying to get us to trust them. Perhaps we'd view them more favourably if they did this. Perhaps we would.

My hand felt warm and tingly where Lyra touched it. Gradually, my skin grew warmer and warmer until it was almost hot, but not uncomfortably so.

One minute I couldn't feel Cavan's presence, the next I could. He was just...there in the back of my mind. This new bond felt no weaker or stronger than the others, but his presence was a comfort. I didn't know how much I needed it until now.

I smiled.

"This is different," he said thoughtfully. "I like it." He sent me adoring thoughts down the bond, which I returned.

"Now you know exactly when she's angry with you." Ryze looked amused.

"Lucky I never do anything to piss her off," Cavan said.

Tavian laughed.

"Are you sure about this?" Lyra asked me. "I can break it again if you like."

I grinned. "I'm sure. It's easier to keep track of them this way anyway."

"Assuming you want to keep track of them," she said dryly. "Rather you than me."

"You don't know what you're missing," Tavian told her. "Khala is someone very special."

"I'm sure she is," Lyra said. "She'd have to be to want to bond with so many men. Vernissa only has three of them, and me. Between we two women, we keep them in line."

"We're pretty good at keeping ourselves in line," Ryze said.

Cavan laughed at him. "I see you're exceptionally good at deluding yourself."

"Everything I do, I do exceptionally well," Ryze told him, unflinchingly. "Good or bad."

Cavan shook his head and rolled his eyes.

"He's telling the truth," Tavian said. "Whatever Ryze does, he throws all of himself into it. We have that in common."

"All five of you do," I said. I could hardly believe I

was bonded to five men. Five strong, intelligent, very different men.

"Did you just say I'm like Cavan, Vayne and Zared?" Ryze asked. He looked like he wasn't sure if he was offended or not, but his amusement didn't falter for a moment.

"In that you are all incredible, yes," I said.

"Yes we are," Tavian agreed. "We're all very special."

Lyra gave us a look and said, "I'll show you to the lunch room. You'll want something to eat before the conversation recommences. That will also give you some time to confer with each other and perhaps you will agree to Vernissa's suggestions."

I would have called them demands, but it seemed like a good idea to keep that thought to myself for now. Somehow, we had to find a way to compromise and get Vayne and Zared out of the stone.

21

KHALA

"We're ready to negotiate a compromise," Ryze said as soon as we walked back into the meeting room. "We'll mediate a meeting between you and the King of Fraxius, so you can discuss your needs and see if he can accommodate them. I can't offer anything else. In that regard anyway."

I glanced over to Vernissa who seemed unimpressed with this compromise.

"What do you mean by that regard?" she asked cautiously.

"I mean that there's no point in returning to the outside world if there's still potential for conflict with the Court of Dreams," Ryze said. "We're prepared to help you find them and negotiate some kind of peace so, wherever you end up, you can be assured it will be better than this." He gestured around the room.

"Even if it means going into the mist?" Cavan asked Ryze.

Ryze's mouth twisted in a barely contained grimace. "Even if we have to do that. Conflict between the two courts will affect all of us. Better to deal with this before it becomes a major problem."

Vernissa glanced at Lyra. The other woman's expression gave away nothing. Either they were communicating through a bond, or they knew each other well enough to know what the other was thinking.

"Very well," Vernissa finally said. "We'll accept your assistance with both matters. However, your people will remain here, in stone."

"No," I said. "You said you'd free them when we came to an understanding. We've done that. If you want us to keep our side of this deal, then you need to keep your word."

I was well aware that might piss her off, but it could take weeks to find the Court of Dreams, and longer to get them to listen. Assuming we found them at all.

Then there was the matter of speaking to the

King of Fraxius. He might not be receptive to speaking to Fae. Zared and Vayne could be stuck in the stone for a thousand years. That was unacceptable.

Vernissa and Lyra exchanged another look.

"How do we know you'll help us after we free them?" Lyra asked.

"Because we said we would," Tavian said. "Ryzellius is a man of his word. If he says he'll do something, he will."

"So will I," Cavan said.

"Me too," I said. "I'll do anything to avoid innocent people dying."

I understood their reservations. They were locked away from the world for so long, it must be difficult to know who to trust. As far as they were concerned, we were strangers who turned up on their doorstep.

Technically, we didn't even knock.

Although, technically there wasn't a door to knock on. Still, we could have been anyone who stumbled upon the cavern. How could they be sure we were who we said we were?

Ryze and Cavan both displayed the arrogance of a High Lord, but so did many other Fae. Dalyth had had arrogance to spare.

"You can send people with us, or come yourself," Ryze said. "I'm sure you must be curious about the world out there."

"You should take a look before you decide to rejoin it," Tavian said. "You might not like what you see. Believe it or not, there are some real assholes out there."

That was all too accurate.

"What will you do if you don't like it out there?" I asked.

"My people have made their feelings clear," Vernissa said. "They don't want to remain here. What we find out there, we'll deal with. We'll adapt. Or the world will have to adapt to us. Remaining here is not a viable option. We're stifling here."

"Will you cull your people on the outside?" I asked.

"If doing so is necessary," she replied.

I didn't expect her to be apologetic, or regretful, and she wasn't. Killing older Fae just for being older was something she endorsed. A decision she made because she thought it was the best thing for all her people.

And yet, I had the impression she was holding onto her leadership by a very fine thread. Her people wanted out of the shadows, and the gods knew what they might do when they got there. Not to mention what they might do if she denied them.

"Do you have an heir?" I asked, without thinking.

"I do but he'd prefer to be a farmer." Her lip curled slightly.

I blinked a couple of times. "Rijal? Rijal is your son?"

She was surrounded by strong men she owned. Why not let one impregnate her, so she could have an heir? It was no different to a man marrying a woman for the same reason. Except men didn't usually own their wives. Or any other woman, for that matter.

"He is," she agreed. "I hope he wasn't too bothersome. He was born with far too much curiosity for his own good."

"He wasn't bothersome in the least," I said. "He seemed to want to live his best life, that's all."

"That's all any of us want," Vernissa said. "Which is why we need your help. Living here was a safer option, but it is far from our best lives. This is merely...existing."

I felt that acutely. When I was a Silent Maiden, I felt like I was moving from one day to the next, always waiting for something to happen. Hoping for something to break the monotony, to change the daily routine.

If I knew what came after, I might have better appreciated the peace in those days.

I would have tried to spend more time with Tyla if I knew our time was limited.

Guilt twinged inside me for not having thought about her for days. So many other things occupied my thoughts, pushing her to the side.

What would she think about all of this? She probably wouldn't believe any of it, and if she did, she'd find it hilarious. Especially the part about me being bonded to five men.

Would things be different between Zared and me if I'd known we'd be here right now? I suspected it wouldn't. The way we came about was right for us, although he'd spent a lot of time frustrated as fuck, and hoping I'd see what was right in front of me.

"No one should go through life just existing," Tavian said. "Life is meant to be grabbed by the balls and lived."

"That's a very interesting analogy," Lyra told him.

He grinned. "I'm all about interesting, especially analogies. Although, that one is literal some of the time."

"I don't doubt that. You say you're an assassin?"

"Former assassin," he said. "Now I just organise other assassins. Although, I have been known to dabble here and there when the need arises."

He gave me a glance and I knew he was thinking about Wornar. I wouldn't regret for a moment if he used those skills on *him*.

"We haven't had need of an assassin for a long time," Vernissa said. "We may have to make use of your services in the future. Or those of your subordinates. Do you own them?"

Tavian laughed. "No, they just work for me. If I tried to suggest I owned them, I might end up dead myself. That would be...unfortunate."

"Very unfortunate," Ryze agreed. "I've become attached to you."

"Thank you," Cavan said as though Ryze was talking about him.

Ryze rolled his eyes, but smiled. "You're all right, I suppose."

"Can we get Vayne and Zared out of the stone now, please?" I asked.

Lyra glanced at Vernissa, who nodded reluctantly.

"If we must. However, if we detect any signs you plan to betray us—"

"We won't," Ryze said firmly.

"Very well. I see no reason for further delay. If you'll excuse me, I have pressing matters to attend to." Vernissa rose and swept from the room, leaving us to follow Lyra.

I STOOD BESIDE ZARED, gripped by a mix of anticipation and anxiety.

Lyra insisted she could free them. I'd believe it when I saw it with my own two eyes.

She stepped forward, her presence almost radiating with raw magic. Her eyes were focused, her expression her usual serenity.

Her hands moved gracefully through the air, tracing invisible patterns. Not the Silent Maidens' hand language, but similar.

I hadn't seen anyone do magic with any kind of gestures before. I didn't know what it meant that she did just now. Maybe it was more complex magic and maybe it was a habit.

Some people spoke with their hands, she removed stone from my lovers with hers.

Whatever got the task done.

The air around us seemed to hum. A tingling energy enveloping the space.

I held my breath. My eyes never left the frozen figures of Zared and Vayne, hoping like fuck that Lyra's magic was enough to shatter the stone.

A surge of energy pulsed through the room, thick enough to feel. My heart leaped in response.

I saw subtle changes in the stone encasing Zared and Vayne, faint cracks forming, bit by bit.

Lyra's focus intensified, her magic swirling around the statues, coaxing them back to life.

A moment of intense silence hung in the air, broken only by the sound of my own heartbeat pounding in my ears. And then, from one moment to the next, the stone began to crumble, revealing the two men trapped inside.

As the fragments fell away, Zared and Vayne took their first gasps of air, their features shifting from rigid to alive and animated.

My breath caught in my throat as Vayne's eyes found mine. A combination of awe, gratitude and pissed off as fuck flashed across his face.

He took a tentative step forward, finding his balance, and then he was standing in front of me, his warmth palpable.

I reached out, trembling, as he pulled me into an embrace, the weight of his arms reassurance for us both.

"Khala," he whispered, his voice filled with relief. "Thank fuck."

Unable to speak, I nodded against his chest, tears streaming down my face. The joy of seeing him free, the overwhelming flood of emotions, threatened to consume me.

As I held onto Vayne, I stole a glance at Lyra. Her face was beaded with sweat, and a mixture of exhaustion and satisfaction.

A silent acknowledgment passed between us. Gratitude for her returning my men to me. And from her, the understanding that I would do what I could to help her and her court.

I mouthed, "Thank you."

Zared joined our embrace, then Tavian, Ryze and finally Cavan, completing our circle of relief.

The echoes of magic faded and the world righted itself.

Silence fell for at least a few minutes until Tavian broke it.

"Thank fuck you two are all right."

I laughed softly, but I couldn't agree more. If somehow Lyra couldn't get them out of the stone alive, a piece of me would have broken. I suspected that might be the point. Either they held my men to ransom, or they relied on our gratitude for releasing them from the magic they, themselves, put into place.

I suspected none of us missed the way we were manipulated, but for now we'd just enjoy the moment.

22

ZARED

*M*y muscles were still stiff as fuck from being stuck in the fucking stone for more than an entire day.

For the first while, I'd tried to kick my way out, or pound my hands against my prison. I quickly realised that achieved nothing. Trying to shout got me nowhere too. I could move my mouth, but no sound came out.

Once I got past my initial fury, I focused on the bond, and Khala's presence on the other end of it.

Eventually, the minimal air made me drowsy and my brain became fogged.

I was barely aware of anything after that, apart from the other men gently making Khala feel good. I was worried they were pushing her to a place she wasn't ready to go, but she seemed to enjoy what they were doing. Just as well, or I'd strangle them myself when I got out of the fucking stone.

"Are you all right?" Khala asked gently.

Of course she'd be thinking of me right now instead of herself. She looked at me like what I went through was a million times worse than what that asshole did to her. Honestly, it wasn't a competition as to who went through the most trauma. They both sucked. We'd get past it.

Working with the people that did what they did to Vayne and me, that was another matter.

I shrugged and winced with how stiff my shoulders were.

"I'm fine, but if I don't ever get stuck in stone like that again, I'll be all right." I managed a slight smile. "That was bullshit."

"Bullshit is a good word for it," Vayne growled. "I had a fucking itch over my eyebrow and I couldn't scratch it. If I was there another minute, I would have gone out of my mind."

"That sounds like a cruel and unusual torture," Tavian remarked thoughtfully. "On the other hand, it might be a fun way to get information out of someone who doesn't want to talk."

"Itch torture, that sounds terrible." Khala grimaced.

I murmured my agreement. Of course right then my head was itchy. Not just mine. I caught Ryze scratching his cheek in the corner of my eye.

"Only a fucked up person would think of using something like that for torture," Vayne said.

"I see you've met me," Tavian said, grinning.

Vayne grunted and went on eating, even though the bread was dense, and the fruit small. He looked like he hadn't eaten for days.

I didn't have much of an appetite, but I chewed on a corner of bread. "We're not really working with them, are we?"

"We have to," Ryze said. He'd explained the agreement they'd come to in return for releasing Vayne and me. "I don't see any reason to stay here past this meal."

"Where are we going first?" Khala asked. "To look for the Court of Dreams, or to Fraxius, to speak to the king?"

I wasn't sure if they weren't both a waste of time. There was no way the humans in Fraxius were going to allow the Fae to move onto their lands.

As for the other court, it could stay hidden as far as I was concerned. They seemed determined to kill us, so excuse me if I didn't want to help them. Same for the Court of Shadows. They could both get fucked.

"We'll look for the Court of Dreams first," Cavan said. "Let's not alarm the humans for no reason. Until both courts can come to some accord, it seems likely they'll remain where they currently are."

"And reaching an accord could take a century," Ryze said. "The present King of Fraxius will be dead by then. Potentially his successor too. Any agreement we make now would be null."

"Vernissa really would have left Zared and Vayne in the stone for a century?" Khala asked.

"It felt like a fucking century anyway," Vayne grunted. "Even with Hycathe and Jezalyn coming to check up on us. Where are they anyway?"

We all turned to him and stared.

"What do you mean they checked up on us?" I asked. "I didn't hear them."

Vayne frowned and stopped eating for a moment. "I don't know. I had a sense they were there. It only lasted for a few minutes. Why? What the fuck is going on?"

"That's a good question," Ryze said. "As far as I know, they're still in the mists. We haven't seen them since they were taken."

Vayne blinked a couple of times. "I guess it's possible I hallucinated, but I could have sworn they were just on the other side of the stone."

"You don't have a bond with them, do you?" Cavan asked.

"Definitely not." Vayne shook his head. "I felt Khala, but this was different. I can't explain it except to say I thought they were there."

"Maybe you had a vision," Tavian suggested. "When you're in the middle of one, they feel real, but they're not."

"Unless..." Khala said softly.

"Unless?" I prompted.

"Unless they found the Court Of Dreams, and somehow their magic projected a dream of Hycathe and Jezalyn into your head," she said. "I don't know if that's possible."

"They're not called the Court of Dreams for nothing," Cavan remarked. "Did they say or do anything? Were they scared?"

"First of all, the Court of Fucking Dreams can stay the fuck out of my head," Vayne growled. "Second, I had the feeling they were trying to tell me something, but I have no idea what. There weren't any words, as such. They were just...reaching out."

He gestured with one hand to indicate he didn't

know how better to explain what he experienced.

"Fuck," Ryze swore. When we all turned to look at him he said, "This more or less confirms that we have to go into the mist."

"Did you have much doubt of that eventuality?" Cavan asked.

"No, but I had hope," Ryze said. "Don't tell me you are any more excited about venturing there than I am. Because if you try, I'm going to call you a liar."

Cavan pressed the back of his knuckles against his lips. "Excited wouldn't be an accurate word, no. Resigned. Wishing we brought an army with us."

"What if we tell Harel and Wornar there are multiple chests of gold and virgin omegas in the mist?" Tavian asked, a mischievous smile on his face. "If they don't come back, we'll know it's not safe for us to go."

"It's highly unlikely to be safe for us to go," Ryze said. "It seems we don't have a choice."

"We don't?" I asked. "It seems to me if we leave, what are they going to do?"

"We made a promise," Ryze said, like that was the end of that. "You saw no sign of Hycathe or Jezalyn? None at all?"

"Nothing," I said. "The only one I was aware of

was Khala." I frowned. "And I knew Vayne was still there too. I don't know how I knew."

"Wishful thinking?" Vayne suggested. "I had the same thought about you. Hoping they hadn't gotten you out and left me the fuck behind."

I regarded him for a moment. "I'd ask if that's something they'd do, but I am, after all, me. If they could have only gotten one of us out, then the choice is obvious."

He grunted. "If I wasn't hungry, I'd throw the rest of my bread at you. Give me a few minutes to eat and I'll happily toss you in the fucking lake." In spite of his gruff tone, the faintest smile tugged at the corners of his mouth.

"We wouldn't have left either of you behind," Khala said unfalteringly.

"Not if we had a choice," Ryze agreed. "For what it's worth, I'm glad we didn't have to choose between you. That would be an impossible choice."

"No it wouldn't, you'd choose me," Vayne told him.

"I agree with Ryze, it's an impossible choice," Khala said before I could respond. "I hope I never have to choose between you, because I want to choose all of you. We're a pack. Whatever happens, we belong together."

"And if anyone goes missing, we'll find you," Tavian said. "We'll leave no stone unturned."

Vayne tossed his bread at Tavian. "The joke is worthy of Ryze."

"My jokes are much better than that," Ryze said, pretending to be offended.

"No they aren't," Vayne said.

"You tell daddy jokes," Tavian said. "But it's one of the things we love about you."

"Thank you," Ryze told him. "I think." He held his hands out to either side.

"You're welcome." Tavian gave him a sideways hug from his chair.

"You know," Ryze said slowly after a minute or two of quiet, "Vayne and Zared should be grateful they were encased in stone underground. If that happened out in the open, for example outside the Winter Court palace, you would have had the birds landing on your head and crapping on you."

Tavian laughed.

"That isn't fucking funny," Vayne told him.

"It kinda is," Tavian said. "But, to be honest, I would have been more worried about griffin attacks out in the open. One well-placed bolt of lightning magic and you'd both be encased in melted stone."

His words brought us crashing back down.

"I'll take bird crap any day," I said. "Or better yet, never getting stuck in stone again. What sort of fucked up booby trap was that anyway?"

I hated to admit to any vulnerabilities, but I was going to have nightmares about being stuck in there for a while after this. I'd never enjoyed enclosed spaces, except my cock in Khala's mouth or pussy. That unease would be worse now.

None of them would blame me if I freaked out, but I'd be pissed off at myself. I was supposed to be the big, tough human priest. Former priest. I'd do the best I could to live up to that, if only in my own head.

"One that would have been worse if we were all encased," Cavan said. "I get the impression if that happened, we'd all be stuck in there forever, or until we died. Whichever happened first. Since the magic seems capable of sustaining life for a prolonged amount of time, we'd soon end up wishing we were in one of the hells instead."

"And you're still working with these people," I pointed out.

"We might be the best chance of brokering peace between the two courts," Cavan said. "And between them and the humans. What they did to you is unfortunate—"

Without thinking, I slammed my fist down onto the table.

"Unfortunate? It was completely and totally fucked the fuck up. How do you know that's not what they're planning to do to everyone up there?" I pointed to the ceiling.

"We don't," Cavan said evenly. "But that sounds to me like a good reason to keep our eye on them. If we walk away, we won't know what they're doing. This is the decision we've made. If you don't like it, Khala may be able to remove your memories again and send you back to Fraxius."

That sounded suspiciously like a threat to me.

"I'm not going anywhere," I told him. "If I have to go along with this, I will. But when all of this goes completely sideways, don't think I won't say I told you so."

"Noted," Cavan said simply. "We'll trust you to keep the closest eye on them of all of us."

"Don't worry, I will," I replied. I was going to watch anyone from the Court of Shadows like a hawk. They wouldn't get away with anything without us knowing about it.

Not one thing.

"*I*t's not too late to walk away from all of this," I said to Khala as I adjusted the straps of my pack. "I've heard there's a nice, secluded beach at the very top of Freid where the fish practically leap out of the water into your hands. We could grow some potatoes and corn and live a simple life."

"Would you really walk away without knowing what happened to Hycathe and Jezalyn?" She brushed hair off her forehead.

She looked weary. Not just tired, but feeling the pressure of everything that happened since Dalyth took the choker off her neck.

I felt the strain myself. A quiet beach sounded like just what we both needed right now.

I decided the straps were as even as they were going to be, and placed my pack beside the door.

"This might make me the asshole, but if it meant keeping you from going through anything else, then I would." I tentatively reached out and took her hand. I stepped towards her slowly like I'd approach a wild animal. Not wanting to scare her, but hoping she wouldn't run.

"As tempting as it is, I can't spend the rest of my life scared." She let me pull her into my arms and rested her head against my shoulder.

"You're the bravest person I know," I told her. "But sometimes the bravest thing you can do is walk away. Let other people deal with the shit. I know we couldn't drag you away, because you want to finish what's been started. Because even though you and Hycathe never got along, you want to make sure nothing happens to her. I've never met anyone with such a big heart. Except maybe Tave, which is strange considering he's an assassin."

"I suppose it's possible to kill people for a living and still be sweet," she said with a laugh. "That is very discordant though, isn't it?"

"Just a little bit," I agreed. It wasdifficult not to adore him. As difficult as it would be not to adore her. I wasn't ready to proclaim my undying love to him, there were strong emotions there. Ones which got stronger every day.

She raised her head and looked at me.

I didn't move a muscle. When our lips met, it was because she initiated it. I had to keep myself from devouring her then and there.

"Zared," she whispered.

"I'm sorry." I pulled back. I wasn't sure what I was sorry for, but it seemed like the thing to say. Maybe somehow I encouraged her to do something she wasn't ready for.

Although, this was Khala. When had she ever let me push her into anything she wasn't ready for?

"Don't be," she said. "Seeing you like that, in the stone... For a while I thought we'd lost you. How could anyone be alive in there? Even when I knew you were still alive, I was scared we'd never get you out. I would have done anything to free you, even if I had to take your place."

I wiped a tear from her cheek with my thumb. "I never would have forgiven myself if you did that," I told her. "I wouldn't wish that on you. On anyone."

All right, I'd wish it on a few people, but I wasn't going to bring them into the conversation. We both knew what I didn't say.

"I know you wouldn't," she said. "But I would

have done it anyway. For you. For any of you. It made me realise how important you are to me. How important it is for me to tell you, and show you."

"I don't want you to do anything you're not ready for," I told her. Even as I said that, my cock twitched. I wanted—needed to touch her. I wanted to bury myself deep inside her and never come out.

"Neither do I," she said. "But I'm not going to let someone stop me from living and making the most of life." She leaned back in and kissed me again. Then her hands were under the front of my shirt and she was pulling it off me.

I let her take the lead. When she pushed me over to the nest, I didn't object. I lay back just where she wanted me and watched her undo my pants and work them down my hips.

She glanced at me and smiled, clearly enjoying being in full control. She knew she could stop at any moment and that would be completely all right. My balls would hurt, but I'd understand. This had to be on her terms.

She freed my erection and wrapped her fingers around my cock. I didn't even try to contain the quiver her touch sent through me. That quiver increased when she licked the tip of my cock, then wrapped her lips around me.

"Am I interrupting?" Tavian said, slipping in the room. "I came in to say the others are waiting, but let them wait."

Khala went on sucking, but her eyes were on Tavian. She was clearly taunting him and enjoying every minute of it. Hells, so was I.

He groaned and adjusted his pants. After a while, he couldn't take watching any more. He stepped over to the bed and lay down beside us. Watching carefully for her reaction, he undid Khala's pants and buried his face between her legs.

Her breathless, little moans nearly made me come undone already. I didn't want this to end yet. Not this quickly.

"Did you bring any of that oil of yours?" I asked, my voice hoarse with lust for them both.

Tavian looked up. His mouth shone with Khala's arousal. "Of course." He slipped off the bed and stopped to kissed my lips, letting me taste her. He flicked his tongue around my lips and inside my mouth.

I groaned. The combined taste of both of them was like nothing else.

"Delicious." I watched his cute little ass as he stepped away, shedding his clothes all the way to his pack which lay in the corner.

I tangled my fingers in her hair, savouring the way her mouth felt sucking me slowly.

I waited until Tavian was back between her legs and reluctantly eased her mouth off my cock. I took the oil and moved around behind him.

I opened the oil and dipped my fingers in. With one hand, I drew Tavian up until he was kneeling, ass in the air, face between Khala's thighs.

I slipped a lubricated finger slowly into his rear hole, stretching him and feeling the warmth of his muscles around me. Another finger joined the first, then a third. I worked my fingers in and out of him slowly, deliberately.

I glanced up to see Khala watching me, eyes half closed in bliss. She was slowly rolling her hips in rhythm to Tavian's lips and tongue.

I slid my fingers out of his ass and replaced them with my cock. I used my hand to position my tip, then slowly pressed myself inside.

"Gods, you're so fucking tight," I breathed. I'd done this before, with other partners but none ever felt as good as him. If I never had anyone else around my cock but these two, for the rest of my life, I'd be fucking content.

Tavian made a sound that suggested he was

enjoying himself as much as I was. As much as Khala was.

Her eyes were locked on me, watching me thrusting in and out of Tavian with slow, firm strokes, while I watched her buck and writhe.

If I wasn't close already, I was after she arched her back and cried out. That and the wet sound of Tavian's mouth on her pussy, drove me right to the edge.

Tentatively, I reached around to wrap my fingers around Tavian's cock. He was as iron hard as me. Bigger than me, but whatever. It wasn't what a man had, but how he used it. And right now, I was using it to drive Tavian and I closer and closer to the precipice.

I slid my fingers up and down his cock in rhythm to my thrusts.

Tavian groaned and went on licking and sucking Khala, pushing her back to the edge.

When she tipped over, I went with her, coming hard into Tavian's ass. At the same time, he came, spilling hot cum over my hand.

Our moans mingled and echoed around the room, sweeter than the temple chorus. The music of bliss and orgasms. Nothing in this world could compare. Not even close.

I sagged over Tavian's back, breathing heavily, heart racing.

For the longest time all I could do was catch my breath and say, "So fucking good."

*N*o one said a word when we finally met up with the others beside the lake.

Ryze took in our flushed faces with amusement.

Cavan looked slightly uncomfortable, with the front of his pants tented. Clearly he felt every bit of it through the bond.

Vayne was off to the side, talking to Rijal. Evidently the younger Fae was allowed to talk aloud to a beta. I couldn't hear what they were talking about, but Rijal stopped the moment he saw me.

"Vernissa is sending him with us," Ryze said. "And them." He waved towards a couple of other Fae. "Willum is one of her bonded mates. Jistun is his brother."

All three had night black hair which hung

down their backs. Where Rijal had brown eyes, Willum and Jistun had blue. Their bodies were slender, contrasting with Rijal's muscular frame. He was one of the biggest, broadest Fae I'd ever seen. Presumably his role serving his mother saw him do more physical tasks than most others.

Willum nodded at me, then gestured for all of us to follow him to the tunnel through which we'd entered. We walked in silence until we passed the spot where Vayne and Zared were imprisoned.

"How do we get back up?" I asked. "We fell down an incline to get here."

"Please don't say there's a staircase back up," Vayne said with a grunt.

"Scared of a little walking?" Ryze asked him.

"Scared, no. Fully aware how far down we came, yes."

Willum gave them both a funny look. "We're going down. A tunnel leads directly to the mists. We don't go there."

"Today you are," Ryze said.

"Today we are," Willum agreed. His expression was so guarded I couldn't guess what he thought about any of this. Had Vernissa told him to go or had he volunteered?

I wasn't going to ask. What went on between them was their business.

It wasn't until Willum illuminated the tunnel before we headed into it, that I realised he was also an alpha. From the scent of them, Jistun and Rijal were both betas.

I fell in beside Rijal as we stepped into the tunnel. "Are you related to either of them?" I asked out of curiosity.

He glanced over to me and signed. "Jistun is my father. So, Willum is my uncle."

"And your mother is bonded to Willum?" I asked. That sounded awkward.

Although, I was in no position to make any judgement. I was bonded to my mother's former lover. Cavan could just as easily have ended up bonded to her. Perhaps it should feel strange, but it didn't. I felt what I felt and I'd never seen my mother and him together. If Cavan found it uncomfortable, he didn't mention it, or show any indication.

Sometimes I wondered if he saw me as a replacement for her, but I put that thought out of my mind whenever it popped into my brain. He cared about me for who I was, not who my mother was.

"Yes," Rijal signed. "My mother and my father..." He searched for the words.

"Don't like each other very much," Jistun finished for him. "We butt heads more often than not."

"Jistun believes we should stay in our cavern," Willum said over his shoulder. "It's not a popular opinion, especially with Vernissa."

"We're safe where we are," Jistun said, a light growl in his tone.

"We're slowly dying out," Willum contradicted. "You and I will be old enough for the culling after the next one. If we returned to the world above, there will be no need for the next culling. Nor the one after that. We can return to breeding young, like we used to."

"Young who will come under attack." Jistun shot his brother a resentful look.

Clearly this was a conversation they'd had many times before.

"Might those who want to remain stay behind in the cavern?" I asked. "While the rest leave for up there?"

They both gave me a look which suggested I'd hit on a contentious, if unifying topic.

"We are one court," Rijal signed. "Where one goes, we all go."

"Where Vernissa orders us to go, we all go," Jistun said. "Whether we agree with her choices or not."

"If she orders you to do something, you just do it?" Ryze asked. His voice echoed as we moved deeper into the tunnel.

"She is our High Lady," Willum said proudly.

Ryze huffed a breath. "It sounds like my people need to listen to you. They could learn a thing or two."

"Or we could teach them the meaning of anarchy," Tavian said with a grin.

"The last thing they need to learn is that," Ryze told him. "There's more than enough anarchy in the world as it is."

"How to say you have no control over your court without saying you have no control over your court," Cavan remarked.

Ryze stuck his middle finger at him. "I have control over most of them. Just not Tavian and Vayne."

"If they don't obey, you should have them culled," Jistun told him. "If you tolerate disobedience, it grows."

"Vernissa has tolerated yours," Willum said.

Jistun immediately looked defensive. "I obey. I only give my opinion when she permits me to do so."

"She permits you too often then," Willum said.

He waved his hand ahead of us. "We continue down this way."

We fell into silence for a while until Tavian broke it.

"The row of skulls that led the way in. Whose were they? Your enemies or your friends?"

"Those who were culled from age," Willum said. "It's their honour to present the way to those who were chosen to come and free us from the caverns."

"So they were killed for us," Tavian concluded. "We're honoured you went to so much trouble, aren't we Ryze?"

Ryze murmured something that may have been an agreement. "I would have settled for a glass of whiskey."

"Me too," Vayne agreed. "At least your ancestors told us which way to go."

"I can tell you where to go any time you like," Tavian teased.

Vayne grunted and rolled his eyes at him. "How about you don't."

Willum gave them a glance like he thought they might be out of their minds.

"In case you're wondering, yes they're always like this," I told him. "Ryze, Vayne and Tave have been together for a long time. They give each other hells, but they would do anything for each other."

"And to each other," Tavian said.

"Speak for yourself," Vayne said. "I don't want to do anything to you or Ryze. Except maybe stab you when you annoy me too much. With a knife, not my cock."

"Cavan and Ryze give each other hells too," I said.

"Do they fuck each other?" Willum asked.

We all gave both High Lords a speculative look.

In the end, it was Tavian who answered. "Not yet, but if they do, I want to either watch or participate."

"Noted," Cavan said simply.

"No doubt you'll be the first to know," Ryze said. "And by first I mean third."

"Fourth is more likely," Tavian said. "Khala would know before I do." He seemed unworried.

"Either way, you won't be unaware," Ryze said. He glanced over at me. "What would you think of that?" He seemed undecided with a measure of hopefulness that I'd agree.

My gaze dropped to the bulge in his pants, before I looked back up again."As long as you both want it, then I'm all for it," I said.

Of course, now my mind was running away with thoughts of seeing them together the way Zared and

Tave were only an hour or so ago. The idea of Ryze on his knees with Cavan's cock in his mouth, or vice versa, made me wet as hells.

"I think she likes the idea," Ryze said. He must have felt my arousal through the bond.

I smirked at him, then noticed the expression on Rijal's face.

"I suppose you don't talk like this if you're not allowed to do what you want, with who you want." I kept my voice low so Willum and Jistun couldn't hear.

Right now, they were engaged in a conversation about something I couldn't make out. Whatever it was, their exchange seemed intense. Their voices were low, but their expressions suggested agitation.

"We talk like that too," Rijal signed. "We talk about when we're above and we can do what we please. There is much speculation as to who might fuck who. Much...teasing?" He looked unsure as to whether his last gesture was one I understood.

"No different to us then," I concluded. "Do you ever... Do alphas ever order omegas to do things? Maybe things they don't want to do?"

He looked horrified. "An alpha knows their place as inferior to all omegas. To order one would be to face culling. There would be no mercy. No sympathy. This would be a terrible crime."

I couldn't argue with that. It certainly deserved to be considered a criminal act. They could get into the growing line to cull Wornar if they wanted to.

"Does that happen above?" He looked concerned, like he hated the idea an alpha could abuse their power in such a way.

I sighed. "Not often, but sometimes. But there are ways to keep it from happening." I quickly explained what Cavan did to me, and that Ryze ordered the same thing of Tavian.

Rijal nodded thoughtfully. "When we return, I'll recommend this to my mother. She will not want to be vulnerable to any alpha from above."

"She definitely wouldn't want to," I agreed. The idea of Wornar doing to her what he did to me made me shudder. Or Harel, for that matter. Either of them may order her to step aside as leader of the Court Of Shadows, and take her place, or the gods knew what else.

"Are we nearly there?" Vayne asked. "By my estimation, we must be close."

"Very close," Willum said over his shoulder.

Indeed, the walls had become rougher, like they were carved by nature and not hand. The air became colder. Something about it felt ominous and uncomfortable.

"We're getting closer to the mist," Ryze whispered.

He didn't need to tell us that, we all felt it. Like we were being watched by something malevolent. Something big. Something that lived in the mist because it could be all but invisible until it struck.

I found my hand wrapped around Zared's. His palm was somehow cold and sweating at the same time. So was mine.

"I feel I should apologise," Cavan said softly. "I hadn't realised they would feel quite like this."

"Apology accepted." Ryze's tone wasn't as light and full of humour as usual. He sounded like he wanted to be anywhere but here.

"Do you have any idea what caused the mists in the first place?" I asked Rijal. Hadn't Ryze said they appeared one day out of nowhere?

"According to Lyra, it's old magic," Rijal signed.

"Yes," Willum agreed. "Something from before the days of Fae. Somehow released back into the world or brought here from somewhere."

"That sounds ominous as fuck," Vayne remarked. "If I haven't mentioned it before, do we really need to go looking for the Court of Dreams?"

"You might have, and yes, we do," Ryze told him. "Don't let the way the mist feels scare you."

"You've let it scare you for quite some time," Cavan pointed out.

"It's not so much the way it feels, as the way..." Ryze shook his head. "You'll understand when you step out into it."

"Which won't be happening," Jistun declared. He stopped dead and pulled out a knife.

Rijal did the same, with an apologetic look to me.

"You're outnumbered—" Willum started to say.

Several figures stepped out of the shadows, all armed. All looking ready to use them.

"Fuck," Zared whispered.

"What the hells?" Willum demanded. He pulled out a knife of his own. "This insurrection nonsense has gone on long enough. Stand aside and you may walk away without being culled." His tone didn't convince me they weren't completely fucked. It didn't seem to convince Jistun and his co-conspirators either.

"There are more of us than you realise," Jistun said. "You feel how the air is in here. It's evil. It's telling us to stay here. They feel it." He nodded toward Ryze specifically.

Ryze raised his hands. "We have nothing to do with this. All we want to do is get out of here. Even if it means going through evil."

I glanced at him. I didn't think he truly believed

the mist was evil. The Fae behind it maybe. The mist itself was no more malevolent than smoke. Bad for you, but without bad intentions.

"Step aside," Willum said. "I will not ask again—"

He was interrupted by Jistun, who lunged forward and drove his knife into Willum's throat. The Fae man's eyes widened with surprise. He let out a gurgle before falling to his knees and then heavily to the ground.

"Let that be a warning that you will not proceed past us." Jistun pulled his knife free and stood with it held out in front of him.

In the corner of my eye, I saw Tavian slip out a blade of his own. With barely any movement or effort, he flicked it. It embedded in the left side of Jistun's chest, killing him immediately.

Tavian had two more knives out before he even hit the ground. "You don't have to be next if you don't want to."

Rijal and the other four insurrectionists all took a step back.

"We don't have to kill any of you." I looked straight at Rijal. "I know you're scared, but we are leaving here. With or without you." Fear sometimes led to people making bad choices. That included dying for no good reason.

"You wanted to leave here," I reminded him. "What happened to your dreams of being a farmer? Your people need you. You're going to be their leader someday. What happens if you die? Your people won't have a leader and you won't get to live your dreams of growing food in the sun. You know what your mother is doing is for the best for the whole court, right?"

I wasn't sure if it was right for everyone, but staying down here didn't seem right either. If nothing else, they deserved the chance to make an individual choice.

"Put the knife down," Ryze told him. "Put it away and let's get on with what has to be done."

Rijal sighed and slipped the knife back into the sheath at his hip.

"Coward." One of the insurrectionists lunged towards him, but stopped when a knife was embedded in the centre of his forehead.

Rijal stepped aside as he toppled and landed with a sickening thud.

"Anyone else?" Tavian asked pleasantly. He seemed to be having way too much fun with this. I should probably not find it as hot as I did, but he really, really enjoyed killing and was obviously good at it. His pleasure was compelling and attractive.

The other three insurrectionists raised their hands and slipped their knives away.

"If you want to go out there, it's your death." One gave us a dirty look, then moved past us and headed back to the main cavern. The other two were close on her heels.

"Are you coming with us?" I asked Rijal. I glanced down at the three dead Fae. Their blood pooled on the ground, but had already started to mingle and dry.

I'd hate to be whoever explained this to Vernissa. Had she felt Willum die? She must have. That kind of loss would burn. I felt for her. She probably felt as though he was ripped away. And for what?

"I will accompany you," Rijal signed.

I wasn't sure if that was his choice because he didn't want to face his mother or because she'd instructed him to accompany us, but I nodded.

"No," Zared snapped. "He would have killed us or let us be killed. How can we be expected to trust him?"

"I say we leave him behind," Vayne said.

Rijal ducked his head. "I have shamed my court. I let my father lead me the wrong way. I should have followed Willum's lead. I submit myself for punishment."

"We don't have time for punishment," Zared said. "I vote he just fucks off."

Ryze and Cavan exchanged looks while Rijal looked at me.

Apparently everyone had different expectations as to who was making the decisions here. I liked Rijal's assumption in general, but not in this case. I couldn't argue against what Zared said about trusting him. I truly believed Rijal when he said he wanted to leave the cavern, but he was quick enough to pull a knife on us.

"He's accompanying us as a representative of the Court of Shadows," Cavan said finally.

"And he's still young enough to do stupid things," Ryze added. "We will keep an eye on him. If he looks like he's going to betray us, he'll end up like them." He gestured toward the bodies on the ground.

"I will not betray you," Rijal signed.

"You say that now," Zared said, taking away any need for me to interpret for Ryze, Vayne and Cavan. "I'd prefer not to end up with a blade in my back while I'm asleep."

Rijal's hand went to the hilt of his knife.

Everyone stiffened.

The tunnel was silent except for the echo of steel

sliding free. Rijal turned his knife around and offered it hilt-first to Zared.

Rijal gestured awkwardly with one hand that it was his only knife.

Zared took it.

"Better?" Ryze asked.

Zared shrugged and put the knife away. "I still don't trust him."

"You don't have to," Ryze said. "We just have to tolerate each other until all of this is over."

"For the record, I agree with Zared," Vayne said. "But it seems the decision is made."

Tavian hesitated for a few moments before putting his own knives away. "Let's get on with it then. Before the rush of killing them fades and I need another hit."

"Things get ugly when that happens," Vayne said. "One time he almost stabbed me in the ass, just to stab someone."

Tavian grinned but didn't deny it.

"If we give you permission to talk out loud in front of Khala, will you?" Ryze asked. "Can you?"

Rijal glanced at me, then shook his head. "I've shamed myself and my court enough. Talking in front of her would be further shame. I'd deserve to be culled."

"He said no," I interpreted. The specifics of what he said didn't matter. The others would have gotten the gist of it anyway.

Ryze nodded. "I had to ask. Now, how do we get out of here? Please tell me there's not another puzzle. That didn't go too well last time."

Rijal shook his head and gestured down the tunnel before he started off that way.

"This is madness," Zared said softly to me. "He pulled a knife on us. The gods only know what else he might have planned."

"I don't think he has anything else planned," I said. "I think he was led astray. He regrets what he did. We've all made mistakes, haven't we? Where would we be if we hadn't given each other second chances? Ryze and Cavan wouldn't be working together. You and Vayne haven't always gotten along. Hells, Ryze basically kidnapped us from the side of the road and made us go to the Winter Court with him. Where would we be if he hadn't? I think Rijal deserves the same second chance." I hoped like hells I wasn't wrong. This could just as easily go very badly.

"I hope you're right, and your soft heart doesn't get one of us killed," he said. "Especially if that someone is you."

He stopped, grabbed my arm and pulled me in for a quick kiss. "I don't want to lose you."

"You won't lose me." I quickly kissed him back, then followed the others. I didn't want to get left behind in here.

Although, even after a session with Zared and Tavian, I wouldn't have minded an hour or two alone in the dark. It was difficult not to be aroused by so many attractive men. I was lucky to have all of them.

"I better not," he growled. "Because if you go, I'm coming with you. And I'm not ready for that for a long time."

"Neither am I," I agreed. We had a lot more living left to do yet.

I shivered. "Is it colder in here suddenly?"

He glanced around. "It feels the same to me. Cold, dark and not my idea of fun."

"It's definitely colder," Tavian said. His eyes seemed to be everywhere, searching the tunnel for I didn't know what.

Ryze raised his hand to stop us all. "It doesn't feel colder to me either."

"Doesn't feel any different," Vayne said.

Cavan shook his head. "To me either."

"Really?" Tavian asked. "It feels like an icy breeze coming from somewhere."

"Yes," I said immediately. "That's exactly what it feels like. Like a cold breath blowing or—"

"Cold fingers," Tavian finished for me. "Reaching. Stretching out towards us." He shuddered. I'd never seen him look so disconcerted before. If he was uncomfortable, then I had good reason to be.

"The mist," Cavan said. "Is it reaching for all of us or just you and Khala?"

Tavian paused and shook his head. "I don't know. It's just reaching." He pointed in the direction we were headed. "It's coming from there." He moved forward, every step slow and careful.

Zared kept hold of my arm as we followed. Evidently he was taking his promise seriously. If I was dragged away by icy fingers of mist, he was coming with me.

The feeling grew stronger and stronger until we reached the end of the tunnel.

Ryze and Cavan raised their hands to illuminate what looked like nothing more than a dead end wall.

There, in the centre was an indentation the size of a hand.

Rijal pointed towards it. "We press that and the door opens. Then we will be in the mist."

"It's not too late to make a portal and go home," Vayne said.

"We can't portal out from here," Cavan said. "I tried. The cavern and tunnels are warded against making one."

Rijal looked at me questioningly. "What is this..." He was clearly trying to think of how to sign the word portal.

I didn't know that one myself. "It's a magical doorway," I explained. "You don't have those?"

He shook his head. "We have the doors that open and close by magic, but not ones that are made from magic." He seemed intrigued, if slightly scared at the prospect.

I didn't blame him. The first time I ever saw a portal it freaked me the fuck out. Considering I'd just seen a bunch of priests die and Fae trying to take my sisters, pretty much everything freaked me the fuck out at the time.

"How do you get out of here unless you go via the mist?" Vayne asked.

"There are other ways that lead off the mountain," Rijal signed. "Long tunnels."

I interpreted for him. "Looks like the quickest way to get the hells out of here is through that door."

I didn't relish the idea any more than they did.

Especially with the way the icy fingers still tugged at me. They were becoming harder and harder to ignore.

Harder still when I felt like they wrapped around my waist and pulled me towards the door.

"Khala." Zared was dragged along behind me.

My hand didn't feel like it was my own. It rose involuntarily to the centre of the door. I slapped my palm against it, then pushed.

The stone door slid slowly aside, and I was ripped out of Zared's grip.

26

KHALA

I heard him shout my name before the sound was ripped away, along with my breath.

I tried to reach back for him, but there was nothing there. Nothing but damp air so cold and thick, I felt like I was encased in ice.

I tried to grab on to some magic. To do what, I didn't know, but I couldn't get a grasp on anything. I couldn't tell which way was up or down. I wasn't even sure if I was still alive, or if this was the portal to one of the seven hells.

Was I dead? Would I be able to tell if I was?

I sucked in a breath. I couldn't do that if I was dead, could I?

I reached out through the bond. Four of my men were frantic, the other, Vayne, was close.

"Vayne!" I called out. My voice was thrown straight back to me, as though bouncing off a wall.

"Khala?" I wasn't sure I'd imagined that, but it sounded like him.

"Where are you?" I still had the sensation of moving rapidly, right up until I hit something that felt solid, but not hard enough to hurt. It was like colliding with a mattress or pillow.

I grunted and flopped to the ground. I placed my hands to either side of me and tried to catch my breath.

"Fuck," I managed to gasp out.

Everything around me was white and thick. I held my arm out as far as it would stretch. My fingers disappeared from view.

I quickly pulled them back.

"Khala?" Vayne called out from somewhere nearby.

"Vayne?" I shouted back.

"Keep talking. I'll find you."

"What do you want me to talk about?" I asked. It was a rhetorical question. It didn't matter what I said, as long as I kept saying it.

"This kind of sucks," I said. "When I woke up this morning, I didn't think I'd end up in the middle of a cloud. That's what this is isn't it?"

"It looks like a fucking cloud," he grumbled.

"It doesn't smell like one." I sniffed the air. "It's like nothing I've ever smelled before. I don't know how to describe it." It was like old ashes, fresh flowers and some kind of spice. "It's strange."

"I don't suppose you know where the others are?" He sounded closer now.

"I think they're right where we left them," I said. "Near the entrance to the cavern. They're all right." As all right as they could be, under the circumstances.

He appeared right in front of my face, making me startle violently.

"Sorry." He grabbed my wrists when I held them up in front of me reflexively, and pulled me to him.

I wrapped my arms around his neck and leaned against him. "There's no point in asking where we are, is there?"

"You can ask, but I don't have any fucking answers." He leaned back and looked up and all round. "This is why Ryze hated the mist so much. It's creepy as fuck. As far as I can tell, it's more or less harmless. Except the part about bringing us here. Wherever the hells here is."

I kept one arm firmly tangled around him and felt around for whatever it was that stopped my momentum. As I expected, it wasn't a mattress or pillow. It seemed like nothing more than a wall of mist, only...somehow more solid than the rest of it.

None of that made any sense, but that was the best impression or explanation I had.

"Whatever or whoever brought us here, this was as far as they wanted us to go."

"For now," he added.

I sighed. "Yes, for now." The gods only knew how long that might last. "Any idea why they want us?"

"Apart from the fact we're both incredibly attractive? Tave or Ryze would probably say it has to do with the blood that runs in your veins. The visions he keeps having suggest he has Court Of Dreams blood. Either Hycathe does as well or they wanted to keep her away from the Court of Shadows. Unless it's Jezalyn who has the blood of one of them." He shrugged.

"And you think my mother has the same blood and so do I," I concluded. "Couldn't they have sent an invitation? I can read."

He snorted bitterly. "That would have been the polite thing to do. Maybe the fuckers can't."

"And maybe they don't want to," I said. "They might have brought us here to kill us."

"If that's the case, they're screwing with the wrong Fae." He smiled. "Killing us won't be that easy."

"I hope you're right," I told him.

"Of course I'm right," he grunted.

"You sound like Ryze," I said.

"In two or three hundred years, you'll sound like him too." He grimaced. "Now, can you portal us out of here?"

"Right." It hadn't occurred to me to try until he said that. Sooner or later it would have. Neither of us were inclined to stand here and wait for something to happen.

I tried to grab on to even a small amount of magic. I half expected it to be as elusive as it was when I was moving.

Instead, I got a rush of power stronger than anything I'd felt before. Winter magic, summer magic and something else. It was like... Nothing I could wrap my head around. Whatever it was, it was new and it was powerful.

I opened a portal in the middle of the mist, trying to reach the door to the tunnel, where the others were. The portal seemed to fight me somehow. As though it would go...somewhere, but it wasn't going to go *there*.

Perhaps it was too close to the wards, or couldn't guarantee it wouldn't open onto one of my men. Realising the latter might be the case, I stopped trying and directed it a different way.

I had no idea where we might end up. I frantically thought about my bedroom at the Winter Court, or the sitting room there. Or the atrium at the Summer Court.

A thought popped into my head just as the portal settled into one spot.

Vayne grabbed my hand and we ran through to the other side.

"All right," he said slowly. "Where the fuck are we?"

I put a hand over my eyes to shield them from the glare of the sun. I looked across grasslands to a forest beyond. Further away still, a castle perched on top of a hill which rose above the canopy.

"I have no idea," I admitted. According to the bond we were a long way from the others.

A very, very long way.

THANK YOU FOR READING! The story concludes in Whisper of Frost and Flame. If you'd love a bonus scene of Vayne encased in stone, you can grab yours here

ABOUT THE AUTHOR

Maggie Alabaster writes reverse harem and, paranormal, sci-fi and fantasy romance.

She lives in NSW, Australia with one spouse, two daughters, one dog, and countless birds.

Sign up for Maggie's newsletter! Sign Up!

Join Maggie's reader group! Join here!

Follow Maggie on Bookbub! Click here to follow me!

Check out Maggie's website- www.maggiealabaster.com

ALSO BY MAGGIE ALABASTER

Brutal Academy

Book 1 Heartless

Book 2 Cruel

Book 3 Vengeful

Court of Blood and Binding

Book 1 Song of Scent and Magic

Book 2 Crown of Mist and Heat

Book 3 Sword of Balm and Shadow

Book 4 Whisper of Frost and Flame

Dark Masque

Book 1 Bait

Book 2 Prey

Book 3 Trap

Saving Abbie

Book 1 Pitch

Book 2 Pound

Book 3 Session

Book 4 Muse

Book 5 Rhythm

Book 6 Encore

Novella Venomous

Saving Abbie books 1-4

Saving Abbie books 4-6 + Venomous

Ruthless Claws

Book 1 Ivory

Book 2 Crimson

Book 3 Elodie

Harmony's Magic

Book 1 Summoned by Fire

Book 2 Summoned by Fate

Book 3 Summoned by Desire

Shifter's Vault

Book 1 Discarded

Book 2 Deceived

Book 3 Disgraced

Book 1–Pursued by Shadows

Book 2 Pursued by Darkness

Book 3 Pursued by Monsters